THE CROSS OF LOVE

Rena had promised herself that she would never tell him of her love, for his sake. And yet the words burst from her, called forth by the intensity of his own emotion. John loved her. He had said so. And nothing in heaven or on earth could have prevented her from confessing her own love in return.

"I love you," he said, holding her away from him so that he could see her face. "I love you in every way that a man can love a woman. You are mine, and I am yours. That is how it has to be. It was meant. It's our destiny. I couldn't fight it if I wanted to. But I don't. I want to love you and rejoice in you all the days of my life. And if you don't feel the same I have nothing to live for."

The Barbara Cartland Pink Collection

Titles in this series

THE CROSS OF LOVE

BARBARA CARTLAND

Barbaracartland.com Ltd

THE BARBARA CARTLAND PINK COLLECTION

Barbara Cartland was the most prolific bestselling author in the history of the world. She was frequently in the Guinness Book of Records for writing more books in a year than any other living author. In fact her most amazing literary feat was when her publishers asked for more Barbara Cartland romances, she doubled her output from 10 books a year to over 20 books a year, when she was 77.

She went on writing continuously at this rate for 20 years and wrote her last book at the age of 97, thus completing 400 books between the ages of 77 and 97.

Her publishers finally could not keep up with this phenomenal output, so at her death she left 160 unpublished manuscripts, something again that no other author has ever achieved.

Now the exciting news is that these 160 original unpublished Barbara Cartland books are ready for publication and they will be published by Barbaracartland.com exclusively on the internet, as the web is the best possible way to reach so many Barbara Cartland readers around the world.

The 160 books will be published monthly and will be

numbered in sequence.

The series is called the Pink Collection as a tribute to Barbara Cartland whose favourite colour was pink and it became very much her trademark over the years.

The Barbara Cartland Pink Collection is published only on the internet. Log on to www.barbaracartland.com to find out how you can purchase the books monthly as they are published, and take out a subscription that will ensure that all subsequent editions are delivered to you by mail order to your home.

THE LATE DAME BARBARA CARTLAND

Barbara Cartland who sadly died in May 2000 at the age of nearly 99 was the world's most famous romantic novelist who wrote 723 books in her lifetime with worldwide sales of over 1 billion copies and her books were translated into 36 different languages.

As well as romantic novels, she wrote historical biographies, 6 autobiographies, theatrical plays, books of advice on life, love, vitamins and cookery. She also found time to be a political speaker and television and radio personality.

She wrote her first book at the age of 21 and this was called Jigsaw. It became an immediate bestseller and sold 100,000 copies in hardback and was translated into 6 different languages. She wrote continuously throughout her life, writing bestsellers for an astonishing 76 years. Her books have always been immensely popular in the United States, where in 1976 her current books were at numbers 1 & 2 in the B. Dalton bestsellers list, a feat never achieved before or since by any author.

Barbara Cartland became a legend in her own lifetime and will be best remembered for her wonderful romantic novels, so loved by her millions of readers throughout the world.

Her books will always be treasured for their moral message, her pure and innocent heroines, her good looking and dashing heroes and above all her belief that the power of love is more important than anything else in everyone's life.

"Never look for love, love will find you"

- Barbara Cartland

CHAPTER ONE
1864

Crows wheeled and circled in the bleak winter sky, while the mourners huddled over the grave beneath. The chill in the air was not more bitter than the chill in their hearts.

What will we do without him? How will we manage?

The man they were laying in the earth had been their vicar and, in some ways, their father. In their tiny, remote village of Fardale, there was nobody else to care for them, and they remembered now that the Reverend Colwell had exhorted them, praised them, chastised, defended and loved them.

Now he was gone, struck down by a chill he'd contracted visiting a sick parishioner on a snowy night.

For a while he'd seemed to rally, then failed again, finally sinking into pneumonia, and fading gently away.

They all felt his loss, but none more so than the pale, distraught girl who kept her eyes fixed on the open grave, and closed her eyes as the first clods of earth hit it. She was Rena Colwell, the dead man's daughter.

Beside her, a much younger girl, wearing a shawl over her head, slipped her hand into Rena's, offering and giving comfort. She had the work roughened hands of a maid of all work.

"Let's get going, miss," she urged.

"Just a few more minutes, Ellie. I want to talk to the curate who read the service. Why don't you go on to the vicarage, put the kettle on and make a few sandwiches? He'll probably want to join us for tea before he leaves."

But when she approached the haughty young man, who'd travelled over from a distant parish to read the service, he made no bones about his eagerness to depart. He preferred the city and was clearly appalled by this backwater village.

"Have you heard anything about who may be coming to take Papa's place?" Rena asked.

"Well, it's hardly the best situation, but there are always plenty of hacks who've lost hope of anything better."

She stiffened at the implied slur on her father, but he blundered on, oblivious.

"So I should think somebody will turn up any day now. It's a pity there's nobody living in that huge house I passed on my way here. A great man always lends tone to a place, besides bringing employment."

"The last Earl of Lansdale died ten years ago," Rena said. "Nobody seems to know who the next one is, or if there's anyone at all. The family may have died out. The Grange has stood empty since then."

"Then it's a bad business. Well, I must be going. I've got dinner waiting for me at my hotel."

Rena trudged home alone through the twilight, her heart heavy. In the kitchen she found Ellie, the only servant the vicar had been able to afford, ready with tea.

The two young women sat together companionably in the kitchen, drinking tea in the fading light.

"He was never the same after your Mama died," Ellie said.

2

"That's true," Rena sighed. "It's strange to think that a year ago today she was still alive. And then she collapsed and died, and something went out of him. He was always very sweet and gentle to me, but I can't help feeling he's happier now."

"What are you going to do, miss?"

Rena gave a wry smile. "I don't know. That curate made sure to remind me that I shall have to move out of here soon. I'm glad, of course. The village needs a parson. But I don't know where I'll go."

"You could be a teacher, miss. You know ever so much."

"Well, I read a lot, but I'm afraid I don't know enough to be a teacher or a governess. I could care for children, but nobody around here is rich enough to hire me. In fact the only thing I'm any good at is keeping house."

Ellie gave a little scream.

"You can't be a housekeeper miss. What would your Mama have said?"

"Mama wouldn't have approved," Rena agreed. "Her family were 'gentry' who thought themselves above a marriage with the clergy. They were very shocked when she fell in love with Papa.

"But I must earn my living somehow, and I'd be glad to hear of any honest employment before I have to leave here."

She gave Ellie a rueful smile. "I'm afraid I can't afford to keep you on – "

"That's all right miss. Mum'll be glad to have me home now our Gladys has married. Besides, it's time I reminded Bert I was alive."

"Bert?"

"The butcher's boy, miss. He'll do very nicely for me."

Ellie departed next morning in search of whatever

3

success she might have ensnaring Bert. Rena was left alone in a draughty, echoing house, knowing that soon she would be homeless.

Reared on the virtues of thrift and industry she immediately set about searching for a situation. Although she'd told Ellie she wasn't qualified to be a teacher she tried to obtain a teaching post. She would try anything that was honest. But it was January, and no school was hiring teachers.

She placed her name on the books of a couple of agencies. One summoned her to an interview in a town so distant that she had no hope of getting there. Another offered an interview twenty miles away. She walked the distance, got caught in a rainstorm and arrived sodden and covered with mud.

On the way home she was given a lift by a local carter, who dropped her a mile from the vicarage. She trudged home, collapsed with a chill and managed to struggle to bed.

She might have died but for the baker's wife who came to see how she was managing these days, found her in bed with a raging fever, and summoned the doctor.

For the next fortnight a group of women took it in turns to care for her and feed her. In her feverish ramblings she relived moments from the past years.

It had been a gentle, loving life. She could remember, as a little girl, riding on her father's back as he crawled round the drawing room on all fours, and she cried "More, more!"

Sometimes Mama had had to rescue him from the little tyrant.

"Your father's tired, my darling."

And Papa had always said, "No, no, my dear. I like to see her happy."

And it had been a happy life, but without excitement. She had once ventured to say so. And dear Papa had been shocked.

"A virtuous woman, my darling child, seeks her fulfilment in the quietness of home, and not – "

How many lectures had started this way! A virtuous woman did not answer back. A virtuous woman endured the misfortunes of life in silence. A virtuous woman turned the other cheek.

"But Papa, there's this horrible girl at school who bullies me, and sometimes I want so hard to smack her."

"A very natural reaction, my dear. But you must not yield to anger. Answer her with calm strength."

She'd tried calm strength and the bullying had turned to mockery. But one day she had answered back, and discovered she possessed a tongue sharp enough to silence bullies. She had not told Papa, but she had suffered agonies of guilt at deceiving him.

"I'm sorry, Papa," she whispered now.

And the baker's wife mopped her brow and murmured, "Poor soul. She's delirious."

For years it had been like that, secretly growing into a firmer and more determined character than was suitable in a clergyman's daughter, and having to hide it from her parents, who would have been appalled.

When she was fourteen a troop of players came and set up their stage on the village green. She had been entranced. Her parents had taken her to a performance, and she had been so thrilled that she had blurted out,

"Oh I would love to be an actress one day!"

They had been devastated. That a child of theirs could even contemplate such an immoral career had reduced them to shocked despair.

Mama had wept. Papa had talked about a virtuous woman.

But because they loved her they soon persuaded

themselves that she was too young to understand her own words. They had comforted and forgiven her.

But Rena had never again confided her longing for a more colourful life, even for outright adventure.

She recovered. Her nurses said goodbye and left her. She came downstairs to find the place empty and her larder filled with nourishing food. She sought them out and tried to thank them, but they all professed ignorance.

Nor would the doctor allow her to mention his bill, which he declared had been paid. For the first time Rena was realising how much the village loved her as well as her father.

It was heart warming, but at the end of two months she still had no job. As far as possible she ate vegetables grown in her own garden, and eggs from the chicken she kept.

Daily she expected a letter to say that a new parson had been appointed, but from the bishop there was only silence. Both the village and herself had been left in limbo.

"What am I going to do?" she asked herself again and again.

Now was surely the time to embark on that adventure for which she had always yearned. But how could she arrange for that to happen? An adventure was something that came to you, and if one thing was for certain it was that no adventure was going to find her in this tiny backwater that the world had forgotten.

The village which was in an obscure part of the country was seldom visited by anyone outside. This was because the great house in the centre of it, which had been there for ten or more generations, had stood empty and neglected for ten years, since the death of the Earl, Lord Lansdale.

Rena vaguely remembered him, an old man who took no interest in the people who lived in the cottages which belonged to him. He employed very few servants in the house and regrettably few outside, so the villagers knew that they could not look to him for employment.

He had no money. The house, known as The Grange, that he had inherited on the death of the previous Earl, had merely given him a place to lay his head. It did not provide the money to keep it going.

"Nor can he sell the house or any of the lands," Papa had confided to her, "because they are entailed. They must be passed intact to the next heir."

"But suppose there is no next heir, Papa?"

"Then it's a bad business, and everything falls to rack and ruin."

Sometimes he had visited The Grange, taking Rena with him. The old Earl had liked the child, and once shown her the tower which perched incongruously high up over the centre of the building.

That visit had thrilled her, but the Earl had grown giddy and had to be rescued, and she was never allowed up there again. Nor was she invited to visit the house again, which made her sad, because it was a beautiful place, and she loved it despite its dilapidation.

Her last ever visit had been made ten years earlier, when she was twelve. The old Earl had died in the night, and his funeral was held in The Grange's private chapel. Like all the other villagers, she had attended. And, like them, she had hoped that soon a new Earl would arrive, put the place in order and bring prosperity back to the neighbourhood.

But it didn't happen. The Grange, the estate, the fields, all fell into a further state of decay. And the people's despair grew deeper.

The only excitement just now was the rumour that somebody had come, or was coming, to open up The Grange. Bearing in mind what Papa had said about entails, Rena wondered if this meant a new Earl.

For a day or two the village buzzed. But then nothing happened, and the buzzing died down.

One day Rena went to her father's study, where he had written his sermons and where she could still feel his presence. As though he were still there, she found herself saying,

"What can I do, Papa? Where can I go, and who can I ask for help?"

She sighed and waited, as if she would hear her father speak and tell her what to do. Then almost as if the words had been said aloud, she found herself thinking of the cross which had been found in the wood, behind The Grange.

She had been about twelve when it had been discovered by some men working amongst the trees. Her father had been asked to inspect it, and had found something that might at one time had been a large, rather roughly made cross but which was now left with only its centre trunk.

He thought the top had somehow got broken. As it was near the stream it had perhaps been washed away. The large piece of wood was thick with mud, but when they washed it clean, they found engraved on it were some words that nobody could make out.

Her father had cleaned the wood until the words could be seen more clearly. He'd given orders for the cross to be driven back into the ground, high above the stream so that the water would not touch it again.

But they were unable to find the missing cross piece, which had made it look a little strange as it stood surrounded by the trees.

"How can you be certain it is a cross?" she remembered her mother asking, as they walked through the wood.

"You'll be as certain as I am when you see it now," the

Reverend Colwell had told her. "It's been cleaned and we can read what is engraved on it."

It was spring and the trees were coming into blossom. Rena, holding her father's hand, had been thrilled to walk through the woods which belonged to The Grange, and had thought what a wonderful place to play hide-and-seek.

At last they saw the tall, impressive piece of wood, that her father was so convinced was a cross. When she drew nearer, she saw the writing on it, and her father had translated:

"YE WHO ASK FOR HELP WILL FIND IT WHEN YE PRAY TO ME."

"That's what convinced me," her father said when he read it aloud, "that it was originally a cross. I think perhaps it was placed here hundreds of years ago, when the house was being built or perhaps even before that."

"It's certainly very interesting," her mother had said. "I only hope the people who prayed there got what they wanted."

"If it has lasted so long, I'm sure they did," her father replied.

He had given his orders that the cross should stay here, and it was still in place ten years later. Now it was the only thing left to which Rena could take her troubles, hoping that if she prayed hard enough some help might come to her.

Perhaps, she thought, it might even be her father telling her to go there.

"It's really a very simple problem," she told herself. "How to stop myself starving to death. What could be simpler than that?"

She often talked to herself in that ironic way, presenting her difficulties with a slightly wry twist. Her father was sometimes a little shocked by what he perceived as her levity. But Rena had found a sense of humour a great help in confronting the world.

She set out now to find the cross. It was spring again, a beautiful warm spring. She didn't wear her best coat, but slipped on the jacket she used in the garden.

She walked through the village until she saw the gates of The Grange, which, unusually, were standing open. So perhaps the new Earl has really arrived, she thought hopefully.

How neglected it was, she thought. It was quite obvious that no one had worked on the drive. When she moved into the fields on one side of it, they, too, had been neglected. It was depressing. But the birds were singing, the sun was shining, and sometimes she saw a rabbit or a squirrel moving through the grass ahead of her.

Just before her were the woods, with the trees in bud. And there was the stream, and beside it what she always thought of as her father's cross, looking incredibly lovely because the kingcups had come into flower at the foot of it. Golden in the sunshine flickering through the trees, they made the cross itself seem to stand out firmly because the wood was dark.

She read again the words carved on the cross which she could see quite clearly, and instinctively she began to pray. As she did so, she looked down at the kingcups, and one side of them she saw a thistle. It was green and ugly and was spoiling one side of the cross.

It seemed dark and mysterious. Then she remembered that she had a pair of gloves in the pocket of her jacket. They were thick and lined with leather.

When she put them on, she attacked the thistle, finding that she had to pull it with both hands as hard as she could before it finally came out.

And then, she saw to her astonishment that attached to the roots were several coins. She picked them up and started to rub away the mud.

Then stared, thinking she must be dreaming.

They were gold.

And there were more of them in the hole she had made in pulling out the thistle. They were ancient, maybe two hundred years old.

And solid gold.

For a moment she was dazzled. Then she took a deep breath and reminded herself sternly that these coins belonged to the owner of The Grange – whoever he was.

She remembered the open gates, the rumour that The Grange had been re-opened. Now was the moment to find out.

She removed two more of the coins under the thistle, then she put the thistle back where she had found it, pressing it into the earth, so that no passing stranger could make this discovery.

First she took the coins from it before pressing it back into the ground.

Then she stood for a moment looking up at the top of the cross.

"Perhaps you have answered my prayer," she said.

Then she almost laughed at herself for being so optimistic.

"If the owner is a generous man he'll give me at least, one of the coins I found for him. Couldn't I just take one – to help me find some work?"

But it was impossible. She was too much her father's daughter to take anything secretly. Every coin must be handed over to its rightful owner.

At once.

Walking out of the woods she began to move through the field, then into the garden towards the great house.

*

It was a long time since Rena had been to The Grange, and she had forgotten how attractive it was.

It was about four hundred years old, a long, grey stone building, stretching to two wings, and with a tower in the centre.

The tower was an oddity. It had been added about a century after the house was first built, and was topped by small mediaeval style turrets, which clashed with almost everything else about the building. But to the people of the village it was a treasured landmark, and they would not hear a word against it.

The house even maintained its beauty despite its poor condition. Many of the diamond-paned windows were broken and the rest badly needed cleaning.

There had been no gardeners here for a long time, but the flower-beds were brilliant with colour. Even the many weeds somehow seemed part of the picture rather than to spoil it.

On a day like this it was hard to remember the rumours that The Grange was haunted. There were old people in the village who said they had seen and heard strange noises when they visited it.

A surprise awaited her when she reached the front door. It was open. Perhaps there was a new owner, and servants had arrived.

"Or maybe," she thought wryly, "it's the famous ghost."

Hearing no sound, she walked into the hall. Like the rest of the house it was in a very bad way, with dust up the stairs that was so obvious that she looked away from it immediately. The passage which she reached at the end of the hall was not much better. The carpets were grey with dirt and so was the furniture.

"Ugh!" she thought.

There was only silence around her.

Then she thought she heard a slight sound on her left, which was the way to the dining-room and beyond that the kitchen. For a moment she hesitated. Propriety dictated that she return to the front door and ring the bell.

But curiosity urged her forward, along the passage. Curiosity won.

As she moved quietly through the dining room she couldn't help noticing that the table wanted polishing and the top of the fireplace was thick with dust. Probably the glass vases on the sideboard were half full of dust she decided. Really this place needed the touch of a good housekeeper.

Then she heard a sound behind the door that led to the kitchen and the pantry. Now she knew there must be someone in the kitchen.

Quietly she opened the door and crept along the passage which led to the pantry, then to the kitchen, from where the noise seemed to come. The door was ajar and she pushed it open. To her surprise she saw a man struggling to light a fire, and obviously not succeeding.

She could see only his back, but the very shape of it was redolent of exasperation and frustration. He'd stripped off his jacket, revealing a tall, well-made frame in breeches, shirt and waistcoat. She contemplated him.

Then something seemed to make him aware of her presence and he spoke sharply, without turning round.

"Perhaps you can make this damned fire burn! I want some breakfast and the coal and wood are conspiring to prevent me from having it."

There was so much resentment in his voice that Rena could not help laughing.

"Let me do it," she said. "These old fires are very troublesome at times."

The sound of her voice made the man turn round. He was young and unexpectedly good-looking, although his face was partly hidden by a smudge of coal. For a moment they both looked at each other with interest and pleasure.

Then he rose and said, "I do apologise. I don't know who you are, but if you could make this fire burn I could have something to eat. I'm ravenous. I've eaten all the food I brought with me last night, and this kitchen has defeated me. In fact the whole house defeats me. Wretched place!"

She couldn't help laughing again, and assumed a shocked tone. "Do you know, sir, that this house has been called one of the most beautiful houses in the whole of England."

"I could think of several things to call it, but that wouldn't be among them."

"Don't let the new owner hear you say that!"

"It's all right. I am the new owner."

"Oh heavens!" she cried. "And I thought you were a ghost!"

He grinned. "A pretty solid sort of ghost. A pretty filthy one, too. Perhaps we should introduce ourselves. My name is John and I'm the Earl."

"The Earl? You mean – Lord Lansdale?"

"Yes. I don't look much like an Earl do I? More like a pot boy, I suppose."

"My name is Rena Colwell. My father was the vicar here until his death. He brought me to this house several times when the old Earl was still alive. It's such a beautiful place, and I've always loved it. Is something wrong?" For his face had fallen.

"Only that if you're the vicar's daughter it wouldn't be quite proper for me to let you light the fire."

"Oh never mind what's proper," she said at once. "Let's just do what we want." Then her hands flew to her mouth. "No – at least – what I meant was – "

"Don't," he begged. "Don't change it. I preferred the first version."

"Well, so did I," she admitted, "but it was the sort of thing Papa used to reprove me for saying. Now, let me do your fire. I shall need some paper – there should be some in one of the drawers of the table. Then I must have some small pieces of wood and matches with which to light the fire."

"I suppose it is what I should have known," the man answered ruefully. "But quite frankly I'm not used to making my own fire or cooking my own breakfast."

"I promise that you won't be hungry for very much longer."

She had to chase some beetles out of the range before she could do anything else. But at last she got the fire burning and the water in the saucepan was hot enough to cook some eggs. The Earl had some provisions, coffee, a little milk, half a loaf of bread and a large pat of butter.

"I have an uneasy feeling that politeness dictates that I should ask you to share my breakfast," he said. "But – forgive me, I'm too hungry to be polite."

"I'm not hungry. I ate my breakfast before I left home."

This was not quite true, because she had merely picked up some pieces of ham left over from her supper the night before. She was making her few remaining scraps of food last.

"I don't think you can be real," he said. "You're a fairy creature who came by magic to save me from starving to death. What is it? What did I say?" He'd seen a sudden change in her face.

"Nothing," she said hastily. His innocent remark had reminded her of the reality of her situation. "I just – thought of something. Go on with what you are saying."

He raised his coffee cup to her in salute. "To the fairy who saved me. I'm very lucky to have found you."

Rena smiled. "I thought actually I had found you. Whenever I've been here before the house has been completely empty, unless someone was thinking of becoming a tenant. Mind you, they always changed their mind as soon as they saw how much had to be done."

"And now you expect me to do it," the man remarked wryly. "But this place is too big and too expensive for me even to contemplate living in."

Rena sighed.

"Oh, must you say that? I have often thought it would be very exciting if the house came alive again and was not left as it is now gradually to crumble until there is nothing left of it, or its beautiful gardens."

"That's a beautiful hope," he said, "But there is one grave difficulty."

"What is that?"

"I can say it in one word. Money! Money to make the house habitable. Money to employ gardeners, farmers, money for horses to fill the stables."

"That would be wonderful!" she exclaimed. "I've always wanted to ride over your land, but as my father had a very small stipend, we could never afford a horse, much as we longed to have one."

"Yes, of course, you said your father was the parson."

"He was parson to the village and of course, this house, for over twenty years. Now when the bishop finds the right man another parson will prevail here and I will have to leave."

There was a note of pain in her voice which the young man heard.

After a moment he said: "If I can afford it, I would do all those things. I would ask you to help me make this house as beautiful as it used to be, when it was first built."

"Oh, how I would love that," Rena answered. "But you speak as if it's impossible!"

"It is. I've been abroad because I was serving in Her Majesty's Navy. When my ship returned to England I learnt, to my astonishment, that they had discovered, after hunting high and low, that I was the only living relative of the last Earl who reigned here. I'm not sure how long ago that was."

"He died ten years ago," Rena said. "I know the search for his relatives has continued ever since, but people had given up hope."

He sighed.

"At first it seemed part of a fairy story," he explained. "Then I realised that what I had inherited was the title itself, and this house and estate. But as for money – not even a pittance."

"You mean you have no money even though you are an Earl?" Rena asked. This was an entirely new idea to her.

"Not a penny. When I was told that this house came with the title, which had not been used for so long, I was, at first, thrilled at the thought of owning land and of course having a home of my own."

He gave a rueful smile. "I didn't think it was possible to be a poor Earl either. I know better now," he added with a touch of bitterness.

"Surely you can sell some of the land, if nothing else," Rena suggested.

"In this condition?"

"Can't you put it to rights?"

"It would take thousands of pounds, and I have nothing, except what I saved out of my salary as a sailor which needless to say, was very little.

"Besides, it's entailed. It has to go to the next Earl, who might be my son, but probably won't be, since I can't afford to marry. In fact, I can't afford to do anything. I haven't a penny to my name."

"But you have," breathed Rena in sudden excitement. "That's what I came here to tell you!"

CHAPTER TWO

The Earl stared at Rena as though she had taken leave of her senses.

"What did you say?"

"You do have some money," she said excitedly. "That's why I'm here." As he continued to regard her with bewilderment she asked,. "Didn't you wonder what I'm doing here?"

"Well – "

"Do strange women pop up in your kitchen every day, cooking you breakfast with no questions asked?"

"I've never had a kitchen of my own before now," he observed mildly, "so I'm a little vague about the normal procedure. But now you mention it, I suppose it is a little strange."

"A little strange?" she squealed, indignant at his annoying composure.

"One of the advantages of being a sailor is that you become ready for the unexpected, what ever it may be. Hurricanes, mermaids, beautiful young women springing up through trapdoors – Her Majesty's Navy is ready for anything."

"I wish you would be serious," she said severely.

"You're right," he said, nodding. "There are no trapdoors here, and you could hardly have come up through the flagstones could you?"

"You – " her lips were twitching, and she hardly knew what to say.

"Yes?" He was suspiciously innocent.

"Nothing. When you can be serious I'll tell you what I have to say?"

"I am immediately serious," he declared, although the gleam in his eyes belied it. "Please tell me how you came to be in my house? Did you break in? Should I send for the law? No, no, I'm sorry – " for she had risen in exasperation. "Please sit down. I promise to behave like a sensible man."

"You shouldn't promise the impossible."

"Oh dear! Dashed! I'm afraid you understand me all too well, Miss Colwell."

She pressed her lips together.

"Please tell me what you wish to say," he said meekly.

"I came because I'd heard somebody was here," Rena said, "to tell you that I found something on your estate which it's only right for me to give to you."

She took out the three coins she had taken from under the thistle, and put them down on the table. The sunshine coming through the window seemed to make them sparkle.

The Earl looked at her in astonishment. Then he lifted the coins and turned them between his fingers.

"These are ancient," he said. "Several hundred years probably. Where did you find them?"

"Underneath a thistle in your grounds. And I brought them to their owner, which is apparently you."

He looked at her curiously. "Did you not think of keeping them for yourself?"

"I told you, my father was the parson here. One thing he never expected me to do was take possession of anything which did not belong to me!"

"My apologies. It's very kind of you to bring me these coins. I'm sure they're valuable. But you know, they won't go very far. What we really need is a few thousand of them!"

"They may be there for all I know," Rena told him. "That's why I came at once to tell you. You should search as soon as possible, in case anyone does what I tried to do."

"What you tried to do?"

"I was visiting the cross."

"What cross?"

"It stands on your land. It was found years ago. They cleaned it up and Papa deciphered the words carved on it. They are an invitation to prayer, so people sometimes go there instead of the church. I found a thistle growing at the foot, spoiling the beauty of the kingcups, so I pulled it out. These were underneath."

"Just these? No more?"

"I don't know, I didn't look further. But there might be, and that would solve all your problems."

He was silently staring down at the three gold coins.

"Will you take me to where you found these? I can hardly wait to know what's really there."

"I don't think you should hope for too much," she said gently. "I have a feeling that the coins were placed there in gratitude by someone whose prayers had been answered."

"Is that why you were there?"

Rena shook her head. "No, I went there to ask for something. Like you I am penniless because my father is dead and I have to find some way of making money," she explained.

He stared. "You're as poor as that? And you weren't even tempted to keep them?"

"Oh yes," she said quietly. "I was tempted." She rose, to silence further discussion of this fact. "Shall we go now?"

21

He was about to make a light hearted comment, but something about her pale face silenced him.

"If you will be kind enough to show me the way," he said, "I would be grateful."

They left the house and climbed down to the woods and the stream, across a rough wooden bridge, grown somewhat precarious with age.

"Why is the cross on my land rather than in the cemetery?" the Earl enquired.

"Because this is where it was found, and Papa thought it should stay there. Look, there it is."

Just ahead of them stood the cross looking strong, dark and impressive amongst the trees.

She walked quickly ahead, and when she reached the cross she knelt down and said a private prayer thanking God for letting her find the money, with all the good it might do for the man who owned it, for the villagers, and perhaps to her too, although she could not, for the moment, see how.

The Earl stood still, watching her in silent respect, wondering what was happening to him and to his whole world.

Only when she had finished praying did the Earl move forward. She lifted the thistle, which he took from her and flung away. Then he bent down and started to pull up the ground round the cross. It crossed Rena's mind that perhaps he would find nothing. As the Earl pushed his hand lower and lower, she closed her eyes and held her breath.

Then she heard him make a sudden sound which was almost a yell of delight.

She opened her eyes. He was looking towards her, his hand outstretched. In it she saw a large lump of soil. Something in it was shining in the sunshine coming through the trees above them.

More coins. For a moment she thought she was

dreaming.

"Your prayers have been answered," he said jubilantly. "And there are probably more if we dig deeper."

"It is true, it is really true!" Rena said almost beneath her breath.

The Earl lowered his voice. "Let's get back to the house. No one must know what we've found or that we've been here. The rest need to be brought up by experts who know how to treat them so that they won't be damaged."

As he spoke he put the soil he was holding into the pocket of his coat. Then, putting his arm round Rena, he took her back the way they had come. Only when they reached the house and went in through the front door, did the Earl speak.

"You've saved me," he said. "At least for the moment, you've saved me from feeling nothing but despair for this house and all it contains." Then he shook his head like a man in a dream. "I don't know how to thank you."

"It's Papa you should thank," Rena said. "Do you really think there will be enough money for you to restore The Grange?"

"I cannot believe our luck is as good as that," the Earl answered. "But even a little money is a tremendous help. It gives me a chance to think. But this must remain our secret."

"Of course," Rena promised. "Once word gets out and you'll have the whole village digging up your land."

"And the only person I want to share it with is you."

Smiling, she shook her head. "It belongs to you."

"Miss Colwell, please tell me something. When you first went to that place this morning, what were you praying for?"

"For a job," she said simply. "I've 'eaten the bread of idleness for the past two months,' and frankly it's beginning to taste rancid."

"Then let me offer you a job, as my housekeeper."

She stopped and stared at him. "You mean that?"

"It's not much of a job. You've seen the place as it is. It would take a brave spirit even to contemplate taking it on? And indeed you are a brave spirit."

"Am I?"

"Everything you've done today – I'm filled with admiration. You could take that huge task on, and defeat it. Oh, wait!"

"What is it?" she asked anxiously, seeing her lovely new job vanishing before her eyes.

"Perhaps your family wouldn't care for you to take such a post. They might think it beneath you."

"Mama's family probably would. They were Sunninghills, and very proud of it."

"You're a Sunninghill? There's an Admiral Sunninghill."

"My third cousin. Or fourth. Or fifth maybe."

"He might object."

She stopped and faced him. "My lord, are you still in the Navy?"

"No."

"Then Admiral Sunninghill's disapprobation is neither here nor there." With a slight dismissive gesture, Rena disposed of Admiral Sunninghill and all his works.

"But you?"

"They ignored Mama after her marriage. I doubt he knows of my existence."

"I won't tell him if you don't."

They shook hands solemnly.

"And your family at home in the vicarage? How will they feel?"

"I have no family."

"Nobody? No brothers, sisters, mother?"

"No brothers or sisters and my mother died last year."

"You're completely alone?"

She nodded. Suddenly she couldn't speak for the tightness in her throat.

"So," he said, "that settles it. Now you're my housekeeper."

"Then my first job should be to ensure that you are well fed," she said, forcing herself to speak brightly. "I think we've already used up whatever was in the house. If you will give me some money, I will go to the shops and buy provisions, although they won't be very grand."

"I'll be thankful for anything," the Earl answered. He put his hand into his pocket and brought out a sovereign. "Will this be enough?"

"Oh, more than enough," Rena said.

The Earl laughed ruefully. "I hope you won't find my stomach is bigger than my pocket, which happens to most people after they leave the Navy."

"I am sure you were well fed in those days," Rena said. "I dare say ships are run very effectively."

"That's true. Everywhere you looked my ship was clean and bright which is something I cannot say about my house!"

"Leave the house to me. Later, when I've seen you fed, I can bring you some vegetables from my own garden. And then there's Clara."

"Clara? I thought you said you lived alone."

"Clara is a chicken. She lays eggs."

"An invaluable addition to our community," he agreed.

Rena collected a shopping basket from the kitchen and hurried out to the village grocery. Luckily Ned, the owner, had been to the town the previous day, and was well stocked.

She went through the shop like a whirlwind, buying in flour, milk, tea, coffee, meat, butter, sugar, paraffin for lamps. It wasn't going to leave much of the sovereign, but she had a hungry man to feed.

"Are you buying for an army Miss Colwell?" Ned asked in admiration.

"No, for the new owner of The Grange."

He stared. "I did hear someone had arrived but – owner? Are you sure?"

"He's the Earl of Lansdale."

"But the family died out."

"Apparently not. It took time to trace him, and he was in the Royal Navy, which is why it took so long to get hold of him."

"That's good news," Ned answered. "And, of course, if he's opening The Grange, he'll have to repair it and that'll be a blessing to us all. There are too many workmen with no work now." He added slyly, "Best not tell him about the ghost, then."

"I wasn't going to mention the ghost," Rena declared primly, for the simple reason that there's no such thing."

"No ghosts?" Ned demanded indignantly, as if she'd deprived him of a treat. "Course there are ghosts. What's a house like that without a ghost?"

"I suppose there'll be a headless horseman galloping through the kitchen while I'm making pies?" she demanded. "Really Ned!"

"Why are you making pies?"

"Because I'm going to be the housekeeper there."

"Parson's daughter? Housekeeper?"

"Even parsons' daughters have to work to live."

"Well, you'll be in the right place to keep him in order. You can make sure he knows what we all need."

There it was, the burden that was to be laid on the new Earl, the yearning expectations of 'his' people, who looked to him for succour and sustenance.

But as she left the shop she was too cheerful to heed its warning.

Since it was early in the year the light was already beginning to fade as she returned to The Grange. So she hastily filled an oil lamp with paraffin and ventured upstairs to the master bedroom.

She soon found it, a grandiose room with painted ceilings and dirty gilt furniture, full of glory at the expense of comfort. A door stood ajar. Pushing it open Rena found herself in a small dressing room with a narrow bed. The Earl's bags were there, and he'd made some attempt to unpack them, but the bed was bare of sheets and blankets.

Further investigation revealed an airing cupboard containing sheets that were incredibly free from moths. She took out some bed linen and conveyed it to the kitchen, lit a fire inside, and hung the sheets on an old clothes horse in front of it.

Then she put a kettle of water on the top. Now everything was warm and cosy, and the Earl, arriving soon after, stopped in the kitchen door and whistled with admiration.

"Now this is what I call homelike," he said.

"Sit down," she said cheerfully. "The kettle will boil soon."

He drank the tea she set before him with an expression of bliss.

"Sweeter than the sweetest wine," he said. "I see you've been busy."

"You're going to be really comfortable tonight. You've done the right thing in moving into the dressing room. I can put a small fire in there, but the big room would have defeated me. Can you watch the pots on the range, while I go and make up your bed?"

She gathered up the sheets and departed, returning a few minutes later to find the meal almost ready.

"The Earl really ought to eat in the dining room," she suggested.

"No thank you," he replied without hesitation. "We'll eat out here. What's the wine cellar like?"

"I've never seen it."

He took the lamp and disappeared, returning a few minutes later covered with cobwebs but with a bottle under his arm and a triumphant smile on his face.

"Glasses!" he intoned. "We'll dine in style."

She fetched some glasses from the dining room, cleaned them, and laid them out ceremoniously beside their plates. The Earl uncorked the bottle with a flourish and filled the glasses with a delicious looking ruby red liquid, and they toasted each other.

"To us!" he declared. "To finding each other, and all the wonderful things that are going to happen now!"

"I wonder if they will!" she sighed.

"They will because we're going to make them. And this magnificent vintage wine is the first wonderful thing. Sip it slowly and with appreciation, for you may never taste the like again."

Together they sipped.

And together they choked.

"*Thunderbolts and lightning!*" he exploded. "What is this?"

"Vinegar," she whispered between gasps. Her eyes were streaming.

They patted each other frantically on the back.

"Miss Colwell, I really am very sorry," he said

hoarsely. "I thought it would have – aaaarh! excuse me – matured over the years. But it's only soured."

"You said I'd never taste the like again," she reminded him. "I only hope you may be right. No, give that to me – " He was about to pour the wine down the sink but she stopped him. "If what it's doing to my insides is anything to go by, it'll probably clean the range very efficiently."

"You're a marvel," he said admiringly.

She poured tea and they both drank it thankfully. Then Rena served the meal and they ate it companionably at the kitchen table.

"The news is getting around the village that you're here," she told him. "They're afraid you'll be scared off by the ghost. I said that was nonsense because of course there was no ghost."

"Shame on you!" he said at once. "What is an ancestral home without a ghost. I think it very unkind of you, Miss Colwell, that you should attempt to deprive me of my birthright in this way."

His droll manner caught her off guard, and she had to peer at him to make sure how to take his words. The gleam of amusement in his eyes was shocking, she decided. But very delightful.

An answering mirth growing inside herself made her say,

"Forgive me, sir. I had forgotten that among every nobleman's patents of nobility a ghost is essential. However I fear that you may find The Grange's extensive choice a little too much to cope with. There's the Floating Lady, the Wailing Lady Anne, the Headless Horseman – or is it the Headless Horse? Well, I expect it amounts to the same."

"You don't mean I might meet them all at once?" he asked in alarm. "I mean, one Headless Horseman plus one Floating Lady, a man can cope with, but the rest – have a

29

heart ma'am."

She fixed him with a baleful eye. "Would you be afraid?"

"Absolutely terrified."

They laughed together.

"As soon as I've washed the dishes I'll lay the fire in your room, and then I'll leave," she said.

"Leave? I thought you were here for good now?"

"I am, that is, I'll work for you, but perhaps I had better not stay here at night."

She blushed slightly as she said this, and could not meet his eyes. The village would be shocked if she, an unmarried woman, were to share the house alone with an unmarried man. Especially such a young and attractive man as he was. But delicacy prevented her from referring to the matter, except obliquely.

Luckily he understood. "Certainly," he said hastily.

"It's strange," she mused. "When I left the house this morning I thought I'd be back in an hour. Now it feels like another world."

He nodded. He'd had that feeling a good deal himself recently.

"So I'll stay tonight in the vicarage," Rena said, "and return here very early tomorrow, to make your morning tea."

He carried the wood upstairs and helped her lay the fire.

"I'll light it myself when I come to bed," he said. "Now I'll escort you home."

She laughed. "In this tiny village. I've walked about in the dark for years."

"Part of the way then."

He took her to the duckpond, from where they could see the church spire, bleak against the night sky.

"The moonlight will show me the rest of the way," she said. "Goodnight."

"In that case I'll take myself to the local hostelry and get to know some of my neighbours. Goodnight."

He strode off in the opposite direction and Rena headed around the pond, to the church and through the cemetery. As soon as the vicarage came in sight she stopped.

There were lights in the house.

She began to run, and as she neared she saw a wagon and trunks being unloaded and taken in through the front door. She ran faster, reaching the door out of breath.

"And who, may I ask, are you?" An extremely refined sounding woman appeared in the hall and challenged her.

"I might ask the same of you," Rena said. "What are you doing in my home?"

"Your home? Our home I think. My brother, the Reverend Steven Daykers, is the new vicar of this parish and this is, I believe, the vicarage?"

"Yes, of course it is, but nobody told me you were coming."

The woman sniffed. "Is there any reason why you should be informed?"

"Well – my name is Rena Colwell. My father was the vicar here until he died in January."

"Then what are you doing here now?"

"I had nowhere else to go. Of course I knew I should have to leave when the new vicar arrived, but I thought I'd be given some warning."

"It seems to me that you've had quite enough time."

They were interrupted by a shout up above.

"Ma, look at these old clothes we've found."

Two girls of about fifteen were standing at the top of the stairs, waving a couple of old fashioned dresses. Rena stiffened as she recognised her mother's clothes.

"They were in the wardrobe of our room," one of the girl's called. "Aren't they funny? There are a lot of other things there too – "

"They'll be mine," Rena said, tight-lipped. "That is my room."

"Not any more," said the woman. "Please remove your things at once."

Rena ran up the stairs and found her room a scene of devastation. Her drawers had been pulled out and upended on the floor. Her small personal possessions were strewn everywhere. The two girls ran after her into the room, staring at her rudely.

"This is ours now. You shouldn't be here."

"Then I will pack my things and go," she said, tight lipped, trying desperately to remember Christian charity. "Please leave while I do so."

Instead of leaving they giggled. One of them picked up a picture of Rena's mother that she kept by the bed.

"What a frowsty old thing." But her smile faded as she saw Rena's face. "Oh, who cares anyway?"

She tossed the photograph on the bed and the two of them flounced out.

Scarcely able to control her temper Rena began to pack up her things, moving like a whirlwind. If she didn't get out of here soon she would do something violent, she knew she would.

In the end her belongings filled two large bags. She took what she could of her mother's clothes, but there was no room for everything, and it mattered more to have the photographs and personal mementoes of her parents.

Then she thought back to the find of the coins, and realised that but for them she would have no place to lay her head tonight. And more than ever she felt that her father was watching over her.

As she struggled down the stairs the haughty woman was standing at the bottom, waiting for her.

"I'm sorry you were inconvenienced," Rena said to her politely. "I shall not trouble you further."

The woman looked her up and down. "I do hope you haven't taken anything that isn't yours."

Rena took a deep breath and controlled herself. "You may be sure that I have not," she said.

A large piece of furniture was being manhandled through the front door.

"I'll leave the back way," Rena said.

"It's up to you."

Some strange noises were coming from the kitchen. Rena discovered what they were as soon as she entered, and received a feathered body almost full in the face. She dropped the bags and clung to it.

It was Clara, her chicken.

"Poor Clara, how could I forget you?" she said. "You're coming with me."

"Put that chicken down," said a tow headed young man. "That's our supper."

"It most certainly is not. Clara belongs to me, and I won't let you kill her."

"What's the trouble?" The haughty woman had appeared again.

"She's trying to take our supper, Mama."

That did it. Rena had born much patiently but suddenly enough was enough.

"Once and for all," she said, "Clara is mine, and I am taking her with me."

She looked at the four of them ranged against her.

"If you take her from me," she said, slowly and

emphatically, "that will be stealing, and I shall report you to the constable."

"Who's to say who it belongs to?" the unpleasant young man demanded. "That animal is parish property, and the constable will say the same."

"No, he won't," Rena flashed, "because he's met this chicken before (she could have bitten her tongue out for the idiotic words). In fact, his mother gave it to me."

"Which means," she added, recklessly casting aside Papa's teaching aside, "that he'll know that this is a den of thieves. Ask yourself how your brother will like that on his first day."

In sullen silence they stood back to let her pass. Still keeping a firm hold on Clara, Rena had to use her other hand to put one bag on the table, fitted her arm over it, and lifted the other with the hand of that arm.

She was horribly aware of what she must look like, staggering out of the house, laden down. It took her an hour to limp through the village to her destination.

But it didn't matter. Nothing mattered except that she had stood up against bullying and won. She could have cried hallelujahs.

Thus it was that Miss Colwell returned to The Grange in triumph, carrying all her worldly goods under one arm, and a chicken under the other.

CHAPTER THREE

Luck was with her. She found the front door of The Grange unlocked, and was able to slip inside. The house was in darkness, so she guessed that the Earl was still carousing in the tavern. That meant she could settle herself in peace.

Dropping the bags, she made her way to the kitchen, keeping firm hold on Clara, who was making contented little mumbling squawks, as though signifying that she felt safe now.

With Clara safely deposited in the kitchen, she lit a lamp and went hunting for a place to lay her head. She could find a proper bedroom tomorrow.

It was dark in the house with only the lamp, and the huge place seemed to echo about her. Suddenly she could hear how full it was of creaks and strange noises. It had stood here for hundreds of years, and seen all manner of history, births, deaths, perhaps even murders. Was it really fanciful to imagine that a ghost or two might walk?

Well, suppose it did, she thought. She was drunk from her victory, exhilarated at giving free rein to something too long repressed in her nature. She had stood up for herself. And she had won. She was ready to take on any ghost.

It felt like being reborn as another person, and she wished there was somebody that she could tell. But who would understand?

He would, she thought suddenly. She had known the Earl for only a few hours, yet instinct told her that she could confide this new feeling to him and he would sympathise.

If only he would return home so that she could talk to him!

Now she had a chance to contemplate him at leisure, which she found herself very willing to do. There was delight in considering his tall, upright body, hardened by years on active service in the Navy.

She liked too the way he held his head, as though there was nobody alive whose eye he feared to meet. That was how a man ought to look.

His face was pleasing with its blunt, good looking features, and the amiable grin that was seldom far from his lips. His eyes were full of warmth and humour, and he seemed to laugh as easily as he breathed.

That had been startling at first. He spoke with a kind of half comical inflection, as though a remark could be amusing or not, depending on how his listener took it.

And Rena had discovered that dear Papa must have been right all along. She really did have a shocking inclination to levity, for part of her instinctively responded to this way of talking with a humour of her own.

Nothing in her experience had prepared her for a man like this. In fact nothing had prepared her for men of any kind.

The only man she had known well had been her father, who had taken life and the world with great earnestness.

Her parents had been devoted to each other. Rena had liked nothing better than hearing Mama tell how she and Papa had fallen in love.

It had been just like Romeo and Juliet, for the Sunninghills had not been at all pleased when their daughter fell in love with the young clergyman who had come to assist the elderly vicar in the church they visited every Sunday.

"Your father was one of the most handsome men I had ever seen," her mother said. "He told me he fell in love with me from the moment he saw me moving into the family pew we always occupied."

"So you both fell in love with each other at the same time," Rena said.

"I suppose we did, but I didn't know it then, because we didn't get the chance to speak for several weeks."

With a shy smile she had added, "Then when we met, he told me later he was so overcome by shyness that he couldn't say more than a word or two."

"I understood because I felt the same. I wanted to talk to him but I couldn't think of anything to say. The first time he came with the vicar to tea, neither he nor I said anything to each other."

"But you were excited at meeting him, Mama?" Rena had questioned.

"So excited that I think I dreamt of him every night until we met again. But that was a long time."

Finally when her parents gave a garden party, she somehow managed, although she could never remember quite how, to show him the strawberry bed. For the first time they had been alone together.

"How long was it, Mama, before he told you he loved you?"

"It seemed to me as if it took a thousand years. I admitted to myself I loved your father but was not certain if he loved me."

"But finally he told you so," Rena said.

"Yes, and I felt as if he took me into the sky and we were together in heaven. I hope, my darling, it will one day, happen to you."

They were certainly two of the happiest people Rena

could ever imagine.

Sometimes she thought they had forgotten her and everything else in the world except that they were together.

But she realised now that it had left her in limbo. They did almost no entertaining, and since her mother's death her father had stayed at home except for his duties. She had met almost nobody.

A curate had stayed with them for a week, and she had sensed that he admired her. Papa had even asked her how she liked him, and reproved her for levity because she had disliked his red hands and wrists, and his habit of sniffing before he spoke.

But she knew he was glad that she did not want to leave home, and the matter was allowed to drop.

Despite her restricted experience she was not quite as unworldly as her father believed. Lacking any other companionship Rena and her mother had grown closer and had many long talks.

She learned that her grandfather Sunninghill had not been a faithful husband. With money to spare, he had indulged himself in the pleasures of the flesh, including mistresses.

Mrs Colwell had considered long before divulging this to her daughter, but had eventually decided that some worldly knowledge was essential, if the girl was not to be left completely vulnerable.

And so Rena knew of her grandfather's scandalous habits and the way he had broken his poor wife's heart.

But her greatest education had come from the kindly way her mother had spoken of these girls.

"They weren't really wicked, my dear, although the world calls them that. They were just sad, misguided creatures who loved him and mistakenly trusted him.

"One of them came to the house once. She was

desperate, poor soul. My father had set her up in a fine house, lavished gifts on her, then thrown her out when she was with child. Even my mother pitied her, and gave her some money."

"Was Grandpapa a wicked man, Mama?"

"He was like many a man, selfish and indifferent, concerned only with pleasing himself. That's why a kind, loving man like your father should be prized. There are so few like him."

In that modest, virtuous household there had been nobody to tell Rena that she was growing into an attractive young woman. Her hair was a pale honey colour, and her eyes which seemed almost too large for her small face, were the blue of the sky.

In fact, if she had been properly dressed and her hair well arranged, a man might easily have called her beautiful.

As it was, when she had seen herself in the mirror recently, she was not impressed. Her illness had left her thin, especially her face, so that her large eyes now seemed enormous.

"I look plain and haggard," she had thought, but without emotion, for what difference could it make to her now?

But suddenly she remembered the Earl saying –

"Hurricanes, mermaids, beautiful young women springing up through trapdoors – Her Majesty's Navy is ready for anything."

He had called her beautiful.

But he was only joking, of course.

But no man had ever used that word in connection with her before. And she couldn't help smiling.

She had come to the drawing room where the lamp showed her a large sofa that might do for a bed, just for tonight. Some moonlight came through the large windows and she decided to return the lamp to the kitchen.

Turning, she headed for the door and immediately collided with a chair that she hadn't seen in her path. It went over onto the wooden floor with a mighty clang that seemed to echo through the house.

She stood listening while the echoes died away. Then there was silence.

She made her way back to the kitchen where Clara was inspecting the floor.

"You'd better come with me," she said. "After tonight I don't want to let you out of my sight. Parish property indeed."

She turned out the lamp, scooped Clara up and returned along the passage to the drawing room. She had left the door open, so that although the passage was dark she could see her destination by the glow of moonlight.

But as she took the final step through the doorway a mountain seemed to descend on her. Clara escaped and flew upwards, squawking horribly.

After the first moment's blind panic Rena fought back fiercely, kicking out with her feet and threshing her arms. She even managed to launch some sort of blow, if the grunt from her assailant was anything to go by.

Then they were on the floor together, rolling over and over in the darkness, each trying to get a firm grip on the other, gasping, thumping, flailing, until at last her head banged against the floor and she let out a yell.

"What the devil – ?" said a voice that she recognised.

The fight had taken them into a patch of moonlight near the window. Rena found she was lying on her back with a hard, masculine body on top of her, and the Earl's face staring down at her with shock.

"M-Miss Colwell?"

At that moment Clara landed on his head.

"Miss Colwell?" he said again, aghast. "It's you."

"Certainly it's me. Kindly rise, sir."

"Of course, of course." He hastily sprang to his feet and reached down to help her up.

"Do you normally attack people who enter your home?" she demanded. She was breathless from the fight, and from strange sensations that were coursing around her body.

"Only the ones who come by night and don't ring the doorbell," he said promptly. "To be honest, I thought you were the ghost."

"Really!"

"Truly, I did. I heard a noise from down here and came to investigate. Then I heard ghostly footsteps coming along the passage, and then some creature came through the door, holding something under her arm. So naturally I thought you were carrying your head."

"I beg your pardon!"

"You were carrying something under your arm, so I thought it was your head. Headless Lady, you know."

"It was not my head," Rena said with awful dignity. "It was a chicken."

"A chicken? Yes – well, I quite see that that explains everything."

Her lips twitched. "You are absurd," she said.

"I beg your pardon, madam! You glide about the house at midnight, carrying a chicken under your arm, and I am absurd?"

"I can explain the chicken."

"Please don't," he begged, beginning to laugh. "I think I'd prefer it to remain a mystery."

"Whatever Your Lordship pleases," she said, beginning to dust herself down.

41

"Don't you think, after this, that you might bring yourself to call me John?"

"Yes, I do. And I'm Rena. And the chicken is Clara. She lays excellent eggs, as you will find."

"I'm moved by this concern for my appetite, but I assure you tomorrow would have been soon enough."

"Yes, but I – oh heavens!" she said, as the evening's events came back to her.

"My dear girl, whatever has happened? I can't see your face properly, but I can tell you're very depressed. No, don't answer now. Let us go into the kitchen and have some tea, and you can tell me all about it."

His kindly concern was balm to her soul. In the kitchen she relit the lamp and he made her sit down on the old oak settle by the stove while he boiled the kettle. She told him the whole story of her arrival at the vicarage, her discovery of the family, and her battle with them.

"I behaved terribly," she said, shocked at herself.

"It sounds to me as though you behaved very sensibly," he said, handing her a cup of tea, and sitting down beside her. "They may not be a den of thieves exactly, but they're certainly a nest of bullies. And the only thing to do with bullies is stand up to them."

"Well, that's what I think too," she said, delighted to find a kindred spirit. "And yet – oh, goodness, if you could have heard the things I said to them."

"I wish I had. I'm sure it would have been very entertaining."

"Oh no, I'm sure that's wrong," she said, conscience stricken. "How can a fight be entertaining."

"Very easily if you have righteousness on your side. Nothing like a good fight. Engage the enemy and turn your ten-pounders on him."

"Ten-pounders?"

"Guns."

"They said – " her voice began to shake from another reason, "they said they'd tell the constable that Clara was parish property, and I said – " mirth was overcoming her, "I said – "

"Don't stop there," he begged. "I can't stand it."

"I said he would take my side because – he'd met this chicken before."

His crack of laughter hit the ceiling. Rena gave up the struggle not to yield to her amusement, and the two of them sat there, holding onto each other and rocking back and forth.

"That's not a ten-pounder, that's a twelve-pounder," he gasped at last. "It must have blown them out of the water. I shall always regret that I wasn't there.

"I ought to have been, of course. I should have walked back to the vicarage with you, and then I would have been there to help. When I think of you struggling back here – and what do you mean by creeping in by stealth?"

"I thought you would still be at the tavern, and the house would be empty."

"No, I didn't stay long. I began to feel rather uncomfortable."

"You mean you felt unwelcome?"

"On the contrary, they welcomed me with open arms. They've decided that my arrival means the good times have come again, that I'll be wanting to restore the house and the gardens and that will provide work for them. I now know the names of every artisan and gardener in the district.

"How could I tell them that I have no money to fulfil their dreams? And my dream too if the truth be told."

"Is it really your dream too?" she asked excitedly.

"Yes. In the short time I've been here I've fallen in love with this place. I'd like to do all the things they want, and live in a house that's as lovely as it ought to be. But not only for my sake. For theirs too."

He gave an awkward laugh. "I've really been thinking only of myself since I inherited the Earldom. I never thought of how it might affect other people, or how they might hope it would affect them. But tonight I was confronted by the reality of other people's lives, and it made me stop and think."

He looked at her ruefully. "Thinking isn't something I've done a lot of in my life. I've done my duty as a sailor, but for the rest I've been heedless, and content to be so. But now – " he sighed. "Their need is so desperate and frightening. It made me feel I should do something about it. And yet – what can I do? Except pray that we find more coins, and they turn out to be worth a lot."

"Yes," she said. "We'll pray."

"So, I escaped, because I wouldn't give them false promises. I came home and started writing letters, until I heard this crash from downstairs."

"That was the chair."

"And why were you going to sleep on the sofa? Do we lack spare bedrooms?"

"I thought I'd find one tomorrow, in the light."

"You can't stay down here tonight."

"Yes I can. And I'm going to."

"Rena, be sensible."

"I am being sensible. Besides, I want to stay with Clara, and I can't very easily take her upstairs."

"Talking of Clara, she's busily pecking my boots. No doubt she thinks she still has to defend you. Will you kindly call your chicken off?"

She laughed and did so, then drained her tea.

"Now, sir – "

44

"John."

"Now, John, please will you be sensible and go to bed?"

He gave her a naval salute. "Ay, ay, ma'am. I'll see you at seven bells."

As she snuggled down on the sofa later Rena remembered how, in her childhood, she'd longed for other siblings, especially a brother. And that was what John was, of course, the brother she had never had; someone she could talk to and laugh with, because they saw the world in the same way; someone who would care for her and let her care for him.

She fell asleep feeling happier than she had for months.

*

She was up at 'seven bells' next morning, and immediately went out to buy fresh milk from Ned. She found Jack, the postman, in the shop, and told him about the new arrivals at the vicarage. "I don't live there any more. I'm housekeeper at The Grange."

"Got a letter for you here," he said, looking in his bag. "And one for The Grange."

She took them both and set off for The Grange. It was a lovely morning, fresh and springlike, and there was a skip in her step.

She found John in the kitchen, triumphant because Clara had laid two eggs.

"One each," he said.

"Two for His Lordship," she replied firmly.

"Fiddlesticks."

"Here's a letter for you." She handed it to him and went in to the dining room to give him privacy while he read it. As she had half expected it was a letter from the bishop, informing her that the Reverend Steven Daykers would soon be arriving to take up his position as vicar at Fardale, and he trusted that she would etc. etc.

"Oh Lord!"

She looked around to see that John had followed her into the dining room, a letter in his hand and a look of dismay on his face.

"What's the matter?"

"We have visitors coming this afternoon. I hope they will only stay for tea, but they might want to spend the night here."

Rena gave a cry.

"That's impossible. You can't let them come!" she exclaimed. "The bedrooms are terrible! Your room is the best of the bunch, but even that needs a wash and a great deal doing to it."

"I shut my eyes when I am undressing, and look out of the window when I am dressing," the Earl said drolly.

"Very ingenious, but we couldn't count on your visitors to do the same. You really must not let them stay."

There was silence for a moment, and she wondered if she'd offended him.

Then he said slowly, "I think I should be honest and tell you that the man who is coming here is exceedingly rich. I met him when I was in India and when he heard – I suppose from the newspapers – that I had come into the Earldom, he looked me up and told me that he was very anxious to see my ancestral home."

"To see your – ancestral – home?" she echoed in a stunned voice.

In silence they both looked around them. They looked up at the grimy ceilings, around at the peeling walls, and down at the shabby furniture.

"He's going to get a shock, isn't he?" she said at last.

"A considerable shock," John said grimly. "I only wish I thought it would scare him off."

"Why do you want to scare him off?"

"Because I have a horrid feeling I know what he wants of me. We met when I was a penniless sailor and he asked me to a dance he was giving for his daughter, to make up the numbers, I believe. Well, I'm still penniless, but now I have a title."

"You mean – ?"

"What this man really wants – and I am quite certain it is what he will say when he gets here, is for me to marry his daughter!"

Rena gave a little gasp. "Why should you do that," she asked, "unless you have fallen in love with her?"

He was silent for a moment, and she felt a strange chill come over her heart.

"No, I'm not in love with her," he said. "But if her father's money can restore The Grange and make the people here prosperous again, it couldn't possibly be my duty, could it? No!"

He checked himself, turned sharply and strode back into the kitchen. Rena stayed where she was for a moment. She was glad that he hadn't waited for her reply to that question, because she was not sure that she would have known how to answer.

After a minute she followed him into the kitchen, and began making his breakfast.

"Why was I even thinking like that?" he asked. "Of course I shan't marry where I do not love. If I marry, it will be to a woman I love, who will make me happy, even if we are not particularly rich."

"I think you're right," she said, concentrating on what she was doing, and not looking at him.

"But you don't think I'll keep to my resolution?" he

asked, shooting her a look.

"I think it could be hard for you if he says he'll restore The Grange. Suppose he gives you enough money to repair it and bring the estate to life again. You could spend your life, in future, as a country gentleman, with of course, horses and dogs to verify it."

There was silence for a moment. Then the Earl walked to the window in the kitchen and stood looking out. Rena thought he was looking at the part of the kitchen garden which was desperately untidy.

There were a few cabbages and onions, but for each one of them, there were at least a dozen weeds.

"I suppose," she mused, "if she loved you, you would perhaps, in time, come to love her."

She wanted to add 'and her money', but thought that sounded rude.

John turned from the window and said in a very positive tone, which seemed somehow to echo round the kitchen:

"I will not sell myself for what they call in the Bible, 'a mess of pottage.' Although it might now be thousands of pounds."

"Well done."

"I would rather starve than find myself married to a woman for whom I have no feelings, and be subservient to a man with whom I have nothing in common."

He spoke almost violently.

"But what else can you do?" Rena asked.

"What did you say?"

"Perhaps you should think hard before saying no." She didn't know why she was urging him to a course of action that she would hate, but there seemed to be a little demon inside her playing Devil's Advocate.

"You must remember how dilapidated the house is already. The villagers thought the roof would fall in last Christmas when we had a great deal of snow. By a miracle, it survived, but I doubt if it will next winter."

He gave her a strange smile.

"Rena, are you urging me to marry for money?"

"No, not exactly, but – are you wise to make a grand gesture, if you might regret it afterwards? This place already means a lot to you. Maybe it will come to mean everything. If you turn down the chance to restore this estate, maybe one day you will regret it."

She found she was holding her breath for his answer. And for some reason it was desperately important.

"The only thing I will regret," he said at last, "is putting money before everything. Rena, I've learned to trust in fortune. I inherited this property after everyone had been quite certain there was no heir to the Earldom. I found you, and you found the hidden glories beneath the ancient cross."

"Yes," she said, glowing with happiness. "Yes!"

He took her hands. "Don't you see, there is more to come. Much more. The future is full of surprises that we can't imagine, but which are waiting for us."

His fervent tone convinced her. This was something he really felt, just as she would feel the same in his position.

"Do I sound like a madman to you?" he asked anxiously.

"Not at all. I know just what you mean?"

"I knew you'd understand. Anyone else would have me put under restraint for such wild talk, but not you. We've only known each other a few hours, and yet already you're the best friend I have. I can tell you things I could tell

49

nobody else. So, keep your hand in mine, my dear friend, and nothing can defeat us."

CHAPTER FOUR

With only time to clean one room they settled on the drawing room. John helped her, and proved more adept than she had feared.

"It's being in the Navy," he said. "A man develops certain domestic skills."

He joined her for tea in the kitchen, while she worked out the refreshments she would serve their guests.

"Tell me more about Mr. Wyngate," she said.

"He's a bit of a mystery man. Nobody knows exactly where he came from, or how he got the money he started with. There's a rumour that his name isn't even Wyngate, but nobody knows the truth about that either. However he started, he made a vast fortune in American railroads."

"You mean he's American?"

"Not necessarily. That's just the first place anybody heard of him. He turned up in America, with money that he invested in railroads, and made a fortune, helped, it is said, by marrying an American lady who had money. She died over there a few years ago.

"Then he came to England and started investing in railways here. He might have been looking for fresh fields to conquer, or he might have been English to start with and returned to his roots, but – "

"Nobody knows," she finished with him.

"Exactly right. He made another fortune here, then took his daughter and went travelling. I met him in India eighteen months ago, when my ship docked at Bombay. He'd taken over the entire Hotel Raj, and was busy competing with the local Maharajah to see who could spend the most money, the most ostentatiously.

"He gave a ball for his daughter Matilda. I did hear that he'd invited the Viceroy as well, but received a polite refusal, which incensed him. In fact it was rather thin of European guests because nobody liked him very much. He made up the numbers by issuing an invitation to the senior officers of my ship, The Achilles, and that's how I came to be there.

"He writes to me as if we'd formed an eternal friendship, but that was my only meeting with him. I've heard a lot about him, but it's the silences that tell the most."

"Silences?"

"If you mention his name people go silent, like birds when a hawk has flown over. He's rich enough to buy anything in the world – or he thinks he is. The trouble is, he's too often right. So many people will sell if the offer is great enough, and now he can't imagine anybody saying no."

"Does the young woman want to marry you?" Rena asked quietly. "What kind of a person is she?"

"I only met her once, at the ball, and formed very little impression of her personality."

"Is she pretty?" Rena asked, busying herself with mixing a cake.

"Not really. She's very quiet, and some men might find that charming. But me – I don't know – she's not for me. I like a woman who has more to say for herself."

"Then you're different to most men," Rena observed, smiling. "Most of them like a woman who keeps quiet and lets them do the talking."

"Indeed?" He raised his eyebrows quizzically. "And may I ask how you obtained this vast knowledge?"

"From my mother," she laughed. "Who obtained it from her mother, doubtless. Gentlemen do not like a chatterbox. Gentlemen do not like a woman who puts forward her opinions, especially if they are contrary to their own. In fact a real lady has no opinions."

"Heavens! What a bore! I must say, it sounds just like Matilda Wyngate. Poor girl. I don't mean to be unkind to her. She'd be the perfect wife for a man of a different temperament to me."

"I feel rather sorry for her!" said Rena. "Perhaps she has no idea what her father is planning."

"Perhaps. I can just imagine him not bothering to tell her. Once he'd made his plans, he's just the sort of man to dispense with other people's feelings as an unnecessary extra.

"He simply can't imagine that there are things his money can't buy him."

Rena gave a sigh.

"I am afraid there are a great many people like that in the world," she said. "Papa used to say that although we were poor, we should always appreciate the beautiful things in life."

"What were they?" the Earl asked as if the way she had spoken made him curious.

Rena smiled. "The sun, the moon, the stars," she replied. "And so many other things, too many to mention."

"That's just the sort of thing you would say," he told her. "I am beginning to think you aren't real, but a part of the magic cross you showed me in the woods. Also the sunshine, which, although you may not know it, is turning your hair to gold."

"Don't let Mr. Wyngate hear you saying things like

that," she reproved. "I understand that it means nothing, but he won't."

John looked as if he wanted to say something, but stopped himself. Then he took a sharp breath.

"Why, that's it! I'll say that you're my wife!"

"John, do be sensible."

"Wouldn't you like to be my wife?" he sounded hurt.

"If you don't take care you'll find yourself engaged to me, and then I'll bring an action for breach of promise, and you'll really be in a pickle."

"Only if I tried to get out of it. I might insist on marrying you. What would you do then?"

"Don't make me laugh when I'm beating eggs," she begged. "It's dangerous."

"Yes, you just flipped some on my nose. Anyway, you couldn't sue me for breach of promise." His eyes were twinkling.

"Indeed, sir? And do you often ask girls if they would 'like to be your wife'?"

"Every day," he assured her. "But I always make sure there are no witnesses. Then there's nothing they can do when I behave like a cad, and vanish."

She was speechless.

He grinned at the sight of her indignant face.

"I learned that from one of my shipmates," he said. "He had a considerable career of that kind. In fact I think he joined the Navy one jump ahead of an outraged father."

"I think you're quite disgraceful. And so was he."

"Yes, he was. Of course it isn't funny if it's real, but I would never actually behave in such a way. I hope you know that."

"What I know or don't know is neither here nor there," she said, concentrating on the eggs. Something in his tone as he spoke the last words had made the air sing about her ears.

"It isn't me you have to impress," she added.

"Well I wouldn't like you to think badly of me, Rena. For any reason."

She regarded him quizzically. "My Lord, since we've met you have set me to work in a beetle infested oven, struck me down and rolled me around on a dusty carpet. Why on earth would I think badly of you?"

He began to shake with laughter, which grew and grew until he put his head down on his arms on the table, and rocked with mirth. Rena stood there, regarding him with delight.

At last he raised his head and mopped his streaming eyes. Then he got to his feet and came round the table, took the bowl from her hand and engulfed her in an enormous bear hug, swinging her round and round the kitchen, while his laughter went on.

"John," she protested, laughing too now, because she couldn't help it. This delightful madman had overwhelmed her with his riotous love of life and her head was spinning, joyfully.

"Rena, you are wonderful," he cried. "Wonderful, *wonderful*, WONDERFUL!"

"John – "

"There isn't another woman in the world who would put up with me as you do. Maybe I ought to marry you after all."

"Stop your nonsense," she said, trying to speak clearly through the thumping of her heart. "You need an heiress."

"Curses! So I do." He released her reluctantly. "What a bore!"

Rena turned away and got on with her work, hoping that he couldn't see that she was flustered.

It meant nothing, she told herself. It was just his way.

And she wasn't used to great-hearted, exuberant men who seized her vigorously in their arms.

"So, you be careful," she said, for something to say. "Or I shall make myself difficult."

"I'm not afraid of you. I'll just set Mr. Wyngate on you. My, that would be a battle of the titans. I think I'd back you against him. All right, all right, don't look at me like that. I was only joking."

She pointed a ladle at him. "That kind of joke can land you in complications," she said, with an unconvincing attempt at severity, "and you have enough of those."

"Well at least I can make a joke with you, without worrying that you'll have hysterics."

"Has it occurred to you that you may be imagining the whole thing? He may not want you at all."

"In our previous acquaintance he kept asking me if I knew any aristocrats that I could introduce him to, because Matilda would grace a coronet. Then the minute he discovers my Earldom he descends on me. How does that strike you?"

"Sinister," she agreed.

"Once he's set his heart on something he never gives up. I suppose that's how he became a millionaire. I feel almost afraid that before I know it I'll find myself walking up the aisle with Matilda on my arm."

"Then perhaps you will," said Rena, almost brusquely. "Perhaps it's your destiny to do what will bring prosperity to the village, no matter what the cost to yourself. Now, would you mind going away? I have a lot of work to do before this afternoon."

This conversation was proving a strain on her.

*

For the visit Rena changed into her severest clothes, and put a cap on her head that hid some of her shining hair.

John was outraged.

"What did you do that for? You look like a servant."

"A housekeeper is a servant."

"Not you. Take this thing off your head."

"Hey, let go." He was pulling pins out. "Give that back at once."

"I will not."

"You will." She stamped her foot. "Right now."

He grinned at her, and the sun came out. "For a servant you're very good at giving me orders."

"John, will you try to be sensible?" She had already fallen into the habit of scolding him like a sister. "While we're sharing the house alone, the plainer I look the better. And Mr. Wyngate will notice."

"Well, if he thinks you're my – well, you know – he won't want me to marry his daughter, will he?"

"Nonsense, of course he will. Where's he going to find another coronet? And what about my reputation in the village? Have you thought of that?

"I didn't even mean to be sleeping here. I was going to stay respectably in the vicarage before a crowd of strangers turned up, throwing me out, making fun of my mother's clothes and trying to steal my chicken – " her voice wobbled.

"Rena, Rena, I'm sorry." His manner changed at once, becoming the gentle, kindly one that touched her heart. He took hold of her shoulders. "I'm a selfish beast. I forgot how much you've had to put up with. My poor, dear girl, are you crying?"

"No," she said into her handkerchief.

"Well, nobody could blame you. Come here."

He drew her against him and wrapped his arms about her, holding her in a warm, brotherly hug. It was the second time that day he had held her close to him, and it threw her into a state of confusion.

"You've been a tower of strength and I don't know what I would have done without you," he said tenderly. "And all I do is make your life difficult. I ought to be shot for my appalling behaviour, oughtn't I?"

"Yes," she mumbled.

He chuckled. "That's my girl. Never mince matters. Heaven help me if I ever get on your wrong side." He tightened his arms so that she was held hard against a broad, comforting chest. He was taller by several inches, and she had a faint awareness of a soft thunder where his heart was.

Then there was another feeling, almost incredible, on the top of her head, as though he had planted a light kiss on her hair. But he released her straight after, so she might have imagined it.

"How do I put this back?" he asked, holding up the cap and pins.

"I'll do it. You go and – I don't know. Practise looking like an Earl."

He grinned. "Do you think I'll pass muster?"

He looked splendidly handsome in a dark suit. But it was his height that was impressive, plus his broad shoulders and long legs.

His face was good looking, but it was more than that, she decided, giving the matter her full attention. It was his proud carriage, the way he carried himself with an air. And then there was the indefinable something in his blue eyes, the gleam of humour and lust for life that was never far away.

It was hard to see how Miss Wyngate would not fall in love with him. In fact, she was probably the one behind this, and her father was acting at her wishes.

Rena had a sense of alarm, as though she could see some terrible danger rushing towards John, and she might pluck him from its path.

But then she realised that she was powerless to do any such thing. They might find more coins, but were unlikely to find enough to help.

She returned to work with a heavy heart.

An hour later there was a sound of wheels outside the front door. They were here at last. She and John had talked so much about them that they had come to feel strangely unreal.

But now they were very real, standing outside, demanding admittance. She felt herself become breathless and a little afraid.

She pulled herself together and tried to assume the demeanour of a servant.

After all, she had wanted to be an actress. This was her chance.

The front door bell rang.

Eyes cast down she crossed the great hall and opened the door.

Outside stood a man in his fifties who, despite his lack of inches, managed to be extremely impressive. He was not particularly attractive, but there was something about him that she had never seen before, an aura of wealth, and power.

It was not only the fact that his heavy Astrakhan coat and gleaming top hat were obviously new and expensive. Nor that his diamond tie-pin was sparkling in the sunshine or that the ring on his finger was also a diamond. It was something more.

She felt it come at her like a blast of air from the furnace of hell. Sheer brute determination to have his own way in all things. Callousness, cruelty, the hardness of rock. She sensed all these things.

Sinister. She had used the word to John almost without thinking, but now that she was faced with the reality she recognised it at once. He was sinister. He was frightening.

And he was something far worse. Rena was a parson's daughter, subtly attuned to the vibrations of another world, and now the hairs stood up on the back of her neck as she recognised evil.

She had never met it before. It had been a theory, a biblical abstraction. Now, at this moment she knew, unmistakeably, that she was in its presence.

Standing beside him was his daughter. She was exquisitely dressed in what Rena assumed must be the very latest fashion. Her clothes were trimmed with fur, her brooch was pearl and her ear-rings were diamonds. Somebody was bent on announcing to the world that she was the daughter of a rich man.

And that same somebody had more money than taste, since Rena's mother, who had belonged to the gentry in her youth, had once told her that no lady ever wore diamonds before six in the evening, and then never with pearls.

"Good afternoon, ma'am."

"My name is Wyngate. Lansdale is expecting me."

His voice was unpleasant and grating, and the way he said "Lansdale" made it clear that he already felt able to command here.

She murmured something respectful and stood back to let them pass. Mr. Wyngate shrugged off his coat and tossed it to her without a second glance. His silver topped stick followed.

Now that he was divested of his top coat Rena could see that there was something strange about his body. He was not a tall man, but his shoulders were very broad and his arms very long. His head, too, was slightly too large for his body. In fact he reminded her of a picture of an ape that she had once seen in a picture book at home.

Then John was there, striding across the hall on his long legs, looking, Rena thought, more handsome than any man had the right to. And it seemed absurd to think that Miss Matilda Wyngate would not fall in love with him.

"Good to see you again Lansdale," Wyngate grated. "You remember my daughter." It was a statement, not a question.

"I remember Miss Wyngate with great pleasure," John said politely.

Matilda smiled up at him in a way that reminded Rena of John's words. "She's very quiet, and some men might find that charming."

It was true. Matilda was no beauty but neither was she plain. Her oval face was pale, her demeanour was shy, and she did have charm.

"I remember Your Lordship very well," she said softly.

"None of that," her father said curtly. "You don't have to 'lordship' him. We're Lansdale's equals any day."

"Indeed you are," John said. "And you are both very welcome to my house. Rena – " he turned to her unexpectedly, "please come and meet our guests."

The idea of a man introducing his housekeeper was outrageous, and plainly Mr. Wyngate thought so too, for he turned cold eyes on Rena.

"This is my cousin, Mrs. Colwell," John continued, apparently oblivious to their astonishment. "She is visiting me to help me look after the house."

There was a twinkle in his eyes as he added: "She will tell you she has found it even worse than she had expected. Rena, my dear, these are my friends. Mr. Wyngate who has been very kind to me and his charming daughter, Matilda who has come with him to see the ruins which have so shocked us."

Rena shook hands with them both, her head whirling.

It was all very well trying her hand at being an actress, but she had not expected the role to change without warning.

Then she realised that John had forgotten one essential stage 'prop'.

A wedding ring.

Where could she find a wedding ring at a moment's notice? Did men ever think of anything?

To conceal the bareness of her left hand she thrust it into the pocket of her dress. And there, to her surprise she found a broken ring which had fallen from one of the pictures. She had taken it down because it was dangerous.

Quickly she slipped the ring on her finger, keeping the broken part well hidden. With luck, it would pass as a wedding ring, if nobody looked too closely.

"I do hope," she said aloud, "you have had a good journey from London."

"An excellent journey," Mr. Wyngate grated. "Fortunately there are trains to this part of the world, or at least to Winchester. After that we had to take a coach, but I fancy that will soon be remedied. The railways are the only modern way to travel, and in time the whole country will be covered with them."

Rena remembered that this man had made his fortune from railways. Clearly he was determined that everyone should be aware of that fact.

But while he spoke he was looking round at the dust and dirt in the hall. Following his eyes Rena thought that it would take at least two or three men a week to get the hall clean and tidy. And he knew that.

She had forgotten that the windows were broken. She also remembered that the stairs going up on one side of the hall were in need of a wash. The carpet on them had almost lost its colour and was torn in many places.

And all the while Mr. Wyngate absorbed these details

he continued talking about railways.

He was a machine, Rena thought, capable of splitting his mind so that it worked in two ways together.

"Now I want you to show me the house, which I can see at a glance needs a lot doing to it," Mr. Wyngate said in a brusque voice.

"I think what you should have first is a little rest after your drive," the Earl suggested. "Perhaps a glass of wine would revive you. Come into the drawing room which is the most civilised room so far. We will show you all over the house later."

"I will not refuse a glass of wine," Mr. Wyngate said. "I am sure Matilda will say the same."

"I think it is so exciting to be in the country," Matilda replied. "I would like to go out into the garden."

"I will be glad to show you," Rena said at once. She was glad of the excuse to get out of Mr. Wyngate's orbit. She found him horribly oppressive.

At the same time she was interested to study Matilda, and Matilda's clothes. Shut away in this quiet place she had had no opportunity to study fashion. Now she realised that crinolines had grown to a vast size. Matilda's was so enormous that it swayed as she moved, and she only just got through the French windows.

She wore a huge skirt of honey coloured velvet, which in itself marked her out as wealthy, Rena thought wryly. Only a woman who could command armies of cleaners could wear something that would dirty so quickly. The blouse above it was white silk, and over that she had a little jacket of matching honey velvet.

But it was her hat that undermined all Rena's resolutions of virtue. It was a perky little creation in the same velvet, worn over her left eye and sporting a feather.

What would it be like to own such a hat? She

wondered. And suddenly her dowdy dress with its narrow petticoats seemed a crime against nature.

"This was once a beautiful garden," she said as they strolled in the sun together, "but now, I'm afraid, only the wild rabbits and the birds enjoy it."

Matilda laughed. "They must have lots of fun playing here with no one to stop them."

"I only hope they appreciate their freedom," Rena said. "I know when I was very young I would have loved to have a place like this to play in. Let me show you the lake."

They moved away together, deeper into the grounds.

CHAPTER FIVE

In the drawing room Mr. Wyngate looked around him. Watching him, John had the same sensation as Rena, that here was a man who noticed everything and calculated exactly how to take advantage of it.

He felt uneasy and troubled. He was a blunt man, a man of action. If an enemy ship had appeared on the horizon he would have known how to deal with it bravely and efficiently. Even ruthlessly. But this situation required dodging, feinting and subtlety. It needed skill with words.

In short, it needed Rena.

And she had abandoned him to manage as best he could.

"So what are you going to do?" Mr. Wyngate barked. "You're not going back to sea, are you?"

"I'm finished with the sea," John said. "I have enjoyed seeing the world, but that's now in the past."

"So you're going to live here?"

"Yes."

"Good. That's how it should be. Houses like this are part of our country's heritage."

It gave John an eerie feeling to hear such words falling from this harsh man's lips. He sounded as though he'd learned them by rote.

"Our country's heritage," Mr. Wyngate repeated, as

though having taken the trouble to learn the correct expression he wanted to get full use out of it, for reasons of economy.

"And our country's heritage must be protected," he went on. "For the sake of future generations. Children. Grandchildren. They need houses like this to remind them of our glorious history. Such places are a sacred trust. They must be preserved at all costs."

His voice was like the cawing of a rook.

"But the place is falling down," he went on. "How the devil do you manage to live here?"

"I have nowhere else to go, and very little choice about how I manage here! I can't sell the house or the lands because they're entailed. They have to be passed on to my heir – intact, which is rather amusing considering the state they're in now."

Mr. Wyngate leaned back against the sofa, and looked pleased.

"That is exactly what I want to talk to you about," he said. "You'd find this place very empty and depressing – if you did not have your cousin with you."

He left the last words hanging in the air, having given them a sly emphasis that made John want to hit him.

"If you mean what I think you do, sir, then let me inform you that my cousin is a most honourable lady, of impeccable reputation and – "

"Yes, yes, yes," the other man said testily. "I'm sure she's as pure as the driven snow. They always are, you know, and if you haven't learned that by now then it's time you did. Never mind her. I don't care what you do as long as she's out of the way when the time comes. I don't want any trouble, d'you hear?"

"I fail to understand you, sir," said John stiffly.

"No, you don't. You understand me perfectly. We're

both men of the world and it's a fair bargain. I'll probably be out of pocket, but I don't mind paying for what I want, as long as I get what I pay for. And I always get what I pay for, because there's trouble if I don't."

John stared at him, feeling sick with loathing at this man who spoke of Rena in such a way. He would have liked to slam his fist into Wyngate's face. The only thing that had prevented him was the reflection that he himself had exposed Rena to this by claiming her as his cousin.

To have inflicted violence on him would had cast further suspicion on Rena, so John clenched his fists and controlled himself with a violent effort.

Wyngate's cold eyes met his.

"I'm quite sure you follow me," he said.

John had the nightmarish sensation that cobwebs were being spun around him, and when he tried to break them he would find that they were made of steel.

Where was Rena?

Why didn't she come and help him?

*

Rena and Matilda had reached the lake, and were wandering around it.

"What a wonderful place for swimming!" Matilda exclaimed.

"If it was thoroughly cleaned up, yes," Rena agreed.

"I enjoy swimming. In America the girls swim almost as much as the men, but that doesn't seem to happen in England. And when you do swim, you have to wear a swimming costume that smothers you, and is thick and uncomfortable. I swim my best when I have nothing on."

"Does your father allow you to do that?" Rena asked, startled.

"He doesn't know," Matilda admitted. "I wait until he's

out shooting or ordering some poor creatures about, then I go out to swim, and I make sure I'm back in my room, dressed like a lady before he returns."

Rena laughed. "I think that's very sensible of you," she said, "as long as he doesn't catch you."

"Yes, he'd be very angry if he thought I wasn't behaving like a perfect lady. And when he says 'lady' he means 'lady with a title'."

"Is that what you want?"

Solemnly Matilda shook her head.

"I'm twenty-four," she said wearily, "and what I want is to stop being dragged about the world, while Papa searches for a title he thinks is grand enough for me, or rather, for him.

"I want to love and marry a man who loves me madly. Then our love would make us happy, whether or not we had Papa's money, or a large house. Without the one you love the grandest house would be cold and empty."

"Then it's love that matters the most to you," Rena said in a soft voice.

There was silence for a moment, then Matilda said:" If I tell you the truth, will you promise not to tell Papa?"

"Of course I promise," Rena replied. "If it's a secret I won't tell anyone at all."

"Very well." Matilda took a deep breath. "I am in love, with a man who loves me as much as I love him."

As she spoke she looked over her shoulder as if she was afraid someone would hear her.

Dropping her voice almost to a whisper, Rena asked: "Does your father know?"

"No, of course not!" Matilda said. "And you've promised not to tell him."

"Don't worry. I'll keep my word. But what are you going to do?"

"I don't know. We're only here because he wants me to have a title. Last month he tried to trick a Duke into marrying me. But the Duke escaped and Papa was lividly angry. I thought he was going to kill somebody. He's capable of it, you know."

"You mean he already has killed someone?"

"No – at least – I don't know. It's only a suspicion and I may be wrong. A man was causing Papa trouble, and he vanished a little too conveniently."

"Good heavens! What happened?"

"I don't know. He just vanished and was never seen again. Papa was trying to get control of a railroad in America, and this man was trying to stop him. Maybe it wasn't Papa. The man had other enemies. It's more that I'm certain he could do something like that. It's there, inside him.

"I've seen him flex his fingers against the air, like this – " Matilda made the gesture. "As though he had somebody's neck in his hands, and would enjoy squeezing it."

Rena nodded. Mr. Wyngate had struck her in exactly the same way.

"But it doesn't last, you see," Matilda went on. "He has a brief spell of being murderously angry, and then he puts it behind him and goes on to the next thing."

"And the 'next thing' is Lord Lansdale?"

"Yes. Papa read about his inheriting the title in the newspapers, and said 'All right, he'll have to do'. He said he was sure Lord Lansdale was in love with me. Well, I could hardly keep from laughing.

"John and I met at a ball my father gave. He danced with me twice and we chatted over a glass of wine. The only thing he could talk about was his ship, but according to Papa he'd been giving me languishing looks, and would have confessed his 'love' but that he had nothing to offer me."

"Did you believe that?" Rena asked, frowning.

"Not for one moment," Matilda said emphatically. "I know when a man's in love with me."

"Do you?" Rena asked, startled. "I mean, even if he doesn't say anything?"

"Good heavens, he doesn't have to say anything?" Matilda said with a chuckle. "It's there in how he looks at you, an inflexion in his voice and – oh, you know."

Rena didn't, but it was impossible to admit.

"Anyway, Papa started 'reminding' me how much I'd liked John. Honestly I barely remembered him, but when I tried to say so, Papa got angry. He wants that title and he won't listen to anyone who says he can't have it."

"If he's got so much money why doesn't he just buy his own?" Rena asked.

"He tried, but the most he could get was a knighthood. Not good enough, you see. An Earl is the least he'll settle for."

"Does the man you love have a title?"

"No, he's just plain Mr. Cecil Jenkins. But as long as I can be with him, I'm happy to be Mrs. Cecil Jenkins."

She spoke bravely, but she also looked over her shoulder.

"It's all so exciting," Rena said, "but I am afraid your dreams may never come true."

"I'm determined to make them come true," Matilda retorted. "But we have to wait a little while. If I elope now Papa would cut me off without a penny."

"Is that ever going to change?"

"No, but we are saving money. I'm getting as much as I can from Papa without him being suspicious. Then when we can afford it, we'll get married and hide until he's forgiven us, which he'll have to do in the end."

"Unless he writes you off, takes another wife and has more children," Rena pointed out.

"Good heavens, you're right. I must make him double my allowance without delay."

Rena was torn between admiration of the girl's courage and a slight feeling of unease at the ruthlessness with which she extracted her father's cash in order to defy him.

"You're shocked, aren't you?" Matilda said, reading her face. "But I'm his daughter and I can be as determined as he is. And how else can I defend myself from him?"

"You can't," Rena agreed. "When the danger is great, you must use whatever defence will succeed. And if I can help you in any way, perhaps hide you, or prevent your father from guessing what you are doing, then you can trust me."

"I knew that when I first saw you," Matilda said eagerly. "I haven't had anyone to talk to for such a long time, and I was sure as soon as I came into the house that the Earl wasn't the least in love with me, no matter what Papa said."

She gave Rena an impish smile. "In fact, I think he'd rather marry you."

Rena stared, her heart pounding. Suddenly she was short of breath. Then she pulled herself together. "You are forgetting that I'm a married woman."

"Oh, nonsense, of course you're not. That story will do very well for Papa, but not for me. Don't worry. You keep my secret, and I will keep yours."

"In any case, I'm sure you're mistaken," Rena said hurriedly. "His Lordship is not interested in me – in that way?"

"Do you call him 'Your Lordship' when you're alone together?" Matilda asked mischievously.

"I really don't see – in any case you've only seen us together for about five minutes – "

"And for all that five minutes his eyes followed you about. I know how he feels about you, but how do you feel about him? Hasn't he ever clasped you in his arms and held you against him? Wasn't it thrilling?"

Rena recalled the hug John had given her earlier that day. It had been kind and brotherly, no more. But then she remembered that other time, when they had fallen on the carpet together, because he had thought she was the ghost. She couldn't banish from her consciousness the feeling of John's hard body against hers, the power she had sensed in him. Matilda was right. It had been thrilling.

But that had been an accident, nothing to do with love. And yet.....

"I hope you find a way to be with the man you love," she said, meaning it.

For a moment Matilda's brave mood seemed to fall away and she sighed. "If he ever knew I was in love with Cecil or that Cecil loved me, he would find some way of either getting him out of the country or perhaps even killing him. Papa has always got what he wanted, and sometimes I think he always will."

"I can imagine. You will have to be very, very clever."

The impish smile returned to Matilda's face. "But of course I'm clever. I'm not Jeremiah Wyngate's daughter for nothing."

*

"Now listen here, Lansdale, if you refuse my suggestion you'll regret it for the rest of your life. You've got to learn to seize your chances, and take what you want in life. It's insane to turn down a good offer when it is made to you."

"You are very kind, but – "

"Never mind all that. I'm offering you an excellent bargain. You'll get your house restored to perfect order, everything that money can buy. What more could you want?"

"A wife I loved, and who loved me?" the Earl suggested lightly.

"Sentimental nonsense! Besides, my daughter has always found you very attractive. She confided as much to me after your last meeting."

"As I recall I talked mostly about my ship. I think she was thoroughly bored."

"Well, of course she didn't show her feelings. Girls don't. But I knew. Now it's time for action."

"You're going much too fast," John said. "Even if I can believe that your daughter had any feelings for me at that ball, it was some time back. She may have other ideas now. Women like to choose their own husbands, not to have them chosen for them!"

"My daughter is different," Mr. Wyngate replied. "She does what I want and she knows which side her bread is buttered!"

The Earl winced at the brutality of this utterance.

"You won't know this place when my men have finished with it," Wyngate said.

"Your men?"

"The men I shall employ to bring it back to its best. Architects, craftsmen, the best that money can buy. The expense will be no object to me."

"But that might not be the ideal way to restore this place."

"What the devil do you mean by that? Of course it's the ideal way. Spending money is always the way. There isn't another."

"That depends on what you're trying to achieve," the Earl said quietly.

"But we've already agreed what we're trying to

achieve," Wyngate said impatiently. "To put the Earl of Lansdale in the setting he ought to have, the setting his ancestors had. Fine lands, a fine house. You'll need a town house as well but that can come later."

"Excuse me," the Earl interrupted him, "that may be your object, but it isn't mine. I can't just think about myself. If this estate can be made to flourish it can bring prosperity to the neighbourhood, give employment to the local craftsmen and traders."

"Good grief, man! What do you want to worry about them for? A man must think about himself."

"But not only himself," the Earl said quietly.

There was a sudden firmness in his voice that alerted Wyngate to the fact that his tactics were at fault. He wasn't a sensitive or subtle man but he was a shrewd one where his own wishes were concerned, and the Earl's words had shed a new light across his path.

"Of course not," he barked now. "A man should share his good fortune with others less fortunate. Noblesse oblige! Very proper. Of course you know your duty to the neighbourhood. But your people will benefit from what I propose. My men will come in and decide what needs to be done, and then employ the locals to do it.

"They'll need to buy provisions from local shops. Some of them will stay at the nearest hotel. They'll spend money, and that's what it's all about after all. Well, that's settled. I'm glad we understand each other."

"You're rushing ahead of me – "

"When you've had a good idea, get to work without delay. That's my motto."

Two shadows darkened the French windows, and Rena came in, followed by Matilda.

"So there you both are," Wyngate cried with a ghastly attempt at geniality that set everyone's teeth on edge. "We were just making our plans. My people will start work on this house next week."

There was a stunned silence from the others. It was broken by the last sound anybody was expecting.

A titter.

A stupid, bird-brained, idiotic titter.

It had come from Rena.

The Earl stared at her. The sheer inanity of the sound, coming from her, took him aback.

"Oh, dear me," she said, covering her mouth with her fingers, and tittering again. "Oh My Lord, how honoured I am to be the first to hear your delightful news. My goodness me, such a proud day for the family."

"Honoured?" he stared at her.

"To be the first to hear of your nuptials. Oh, I declare! Oh my, oh my!"

He wondered if she had taken leave of her senses.

"You are mistaken, Mrs. Colwell," the Earl said formally. "It is far too early to speak of nuptials. Miss Wyngate and I – " he bowed in Matilda's direction, "are merely going to get to know each other."

"Naturally that will happen before any announcement," Rena giggled, contriving to sound totally witless. "But there can be no doubt that there will be an announcement."

"Indeed?" John said frostily.

"Why yes, indeed. If a gentleman like Mr. Wyngate intends to start work which – forgive me – he knows you cannot pay for – then he is certainly doing so for his daughter's husband. Who else would he be doing it for?

"What I mean is that should the wedding – by some accident – not take place, he could send you a bill for the whole cost of the repairs, could he not? Or perhaps a suit for breach of promise of marriage?"

Her eyes were wide and suspiciously innocent, fixed on his face.

"And so you see, once the workmen have arrived, it's all settled, isn't it?" she asked, tittering again. "I mean, there would be no going back. Even if you wanted to. Which of course, you wouldn't. But if you did – you couldn't – because of the witnesses, d'you see? Oh dear, I'm expressing myself very badly – "

"On the contrary," said the Earl. "You have expressed yourself perfectly."

Mr. Wyngate looked murderous.

"Get rid of this silly woman," he snapped.

"You're perfectly right," the Earl said. "Mrs. Colwell, you have leapt to a false conclusion. No nuptials are planned, and no workmen will be coming to this house, next week or at any other time."

"In my opinion it would be better if they start immediately," Wyngate grated.

"And in my opinion it would be better if they did not," the Earl said flatly.

Wyngate changed tack.

"Now, Lansdale, you don't want to listen to these female fantasies. You can't imagine that I would – "

"I don't know what you would do," the Earl said. "But the arrival of your men would place me in an equivocal position. My cousin is certainly right about that, and I would hate to attach any scandal to the family name, just as I am sure you would dislike any misunderstandings."

"Misunderstandings can be sorted out," Wyngate snapped.

"But how much better if they don't occur in the first place!" the Earl said smoothly. "Now, shall we have some tea?"

"Don't bother," Wyngate said. "It's time we were going. I told that coachman to wait in the grounds, so I suppose he's still there."

"I'll summon him," Rena said.

"I would have liked some tea," Matilda said mildly.

"Shut up!" her father told her.

In no time the carriage was at the front door waiting for them. The coachman pulled down the step and opened the door. Matilda stepped in, followed by her father.

But before he entered the coach Wyngate turned back to face Rena and the Earl, standing on the step.

"I've never set my heart on anything I didn't get," he grated. "I'll be seeing you again very shortly."

Then he looked directly at Rena. It was a malevolent look, like a blast of icy wind. It told her that he wasn't fooled. He knew exactly what she had done, and how she had done it. And she would be made to pay for it.

All this was in the silent, deadly gaze that he turned on her.

Then he got into the carriage and slammed the door.

CHAPTER SIX

"Thank goodness for you," John said somberly as they turned back into the house. "If you hadn't come in when you did –" He shuddered. "Rena I hardly recognised you, talking in that half witted fashion."

"But you understood what I was saying?"

"Yes. I would have been trapped. I can see it now, but then everything was strangely foggy. I don't understand it."

"He was weaving wicked spells around you," said Rena.

"That was exactly how it felt. All the time he was talking I knew there was something wrong, but I couldn't see what it was because my mind seemed to be full of cobwebs. It was as though he had mesmerised me. But then you came in and blew the cobwebs away."

He grinned. "You were brilliant. You sounded like the silliest woman in the world, not at all like my Rena."

She smiled. "Sometimes it's easier to say things if people think you're too stupid to be taken seriously. I didn't want to denounce him openly as a scoundrel in case you wanted to go along with his plan."

"You think I'd do that?"

"You need money."

"And you expect me to marry for it?"

"I expect you to remember that the village is relying on

you," she said quietly. "But I'm glad you're not turning to Wyngate. He's evil."

"Yes, I felt that force in him too. But good vanquished evil." He gave her a tender look.

"For the moment," she said in a brooding voice. "But he will come back. He isn't going to give up."

She would have liked to tell him that Matilda had another lover, and would fight the marriage as strongly as they. But she had given Matilda her word not to speak of Cecil, so she contented herself with saying,

"Matilda may give him a shock. She isn't as docile as he thinks. She's very much his daughter. She told me that twice, and it's true."

"Did she tell you anything else?"

"Nothing that I can repeat. But we're on the same side. Let's go and have some tea."

In the kitchen they ate the cakes she had prepared and she said,

"Whatever possessed you to invent that story about my being your married cousin?"

"I was trying to be helpful," he said, aggrieved. "You were so worried about your reputation."

"But everyone knows me in this village. They know my name's Colwell because of my father, not my non-existent husband. Matilda didn't believe a word of it. And neither did he, I shouldn't think."

"Hang him and what he thinks! I'm sorry. That's just not the sort of thing I'm very good at."

"You're more of a man of action," she said, smiling and forgiving him.

"Definitely. When it comes to words I just tie myself in knots."

"You know," she said thoughtfully, "I think we should

go out tonight, looking for coins. There's going to be a full moon, and you need to know your exact position. You might be a millionaire without knowing it. John?"

He was staring into space, but he came back with a start.

"Sorry, yes we'll go out tonight."

"You were in a dream world. Wyngate didn't really mesmerise you, did he?"

"No, but I was trying to think where I've seen him before."

"In India."

"No, before that. He reminds me of someone."

"Probably a picture of the devil," Rena said tartly.

"No, it's a real person – if only I could think who it is."

"Don't dwell on it," she advised. "The worst thing you can do is brood about that man. Don't let him into your mind, because once he's in there, you'll never get him out."

"I've never heard you speak like that before," John said. "It's as though you were looking into another world."

"I suppose I am. I'm looking into hell, and I see him there. He belongs there, and he'll take us all with him if we give him the chance."

"Then we won't," John assured her fervently. "Now stop work and go and take some rest, for we have a busy night ahead."

*

As Rena had said there was a full moon that night, but by eleven o'clock the sky was full of storm clouds and a sharp wind was getting up.

"Would you rather leave it until tomorrow?" John asked.

"I don't think that would be safe. And who needs a moon? We'll take a lamp."

Armed with the lamp and pulling their cloaks about them they left the house and made their way through the windy garden. Moving cautiously, they crossed the old bridge over the stream, and slipped into the woods.

The wind seemed to grow fiercer every moment, and it was a relief to get among the trees, which offered some protection. At the same time the howling through the leaves and branches created an eerie effect.

"I shall be glad to get back," said John. "This is too much like a storm at sea for my liking."

As if in agreement there was a flash of lightning, soon followed by a distant roar of thunder.

"Let's get this finished quickly before the rain comes," John said.

Hand in hand they made their way between the swaying trees, until at last they saw the cross, monumental and impressive in the gloom. At that moment there was another flash of lightning, illuminating the cross that reared up before them, seeming to tower high into the sky. Then it was plunged back into darkness.

John had brought a large knife, and while Rena held the lamp, he used this to dig into the ground. When he'd loosened some earth he plunged his hands in, feeling frantically about, then pulling the loose earth aside. She brought the lamp closer, while they both desperately sought the gleam of gold.

But no yellow shone through the gloom.

John groaned aloud and plunged his hands back into the earth.

"There has to be something," he said. "There has to be – what's this?"

"Have you found anything?"

"Yes, but I don't think it's anything much."

He brought out his hand and raised it to the lamp, so

that she could see a small, leather purse. Opening it, he showed her another coin.

And I think there's another one in there," he said. "But that's all."

They searched a little longer, but found nothing else.

"Well, at least you gained something," she said, trying to cheer him. "It was worth trying."

"What did you say?" he shouted, getting to his feet and trying to make himself heard over the wind.

She raised her voice and repeated the words, also shouting over the wind.

"Let's go home," he yelled.

"Yes, let's."

In that moment the lightning split the sky again, seeming to streak down to earth, and there, in a narrow space between the trees, she saw Wyngate.

She caught her breath at the sight of that wicked, brooding presence, standing so terribly still. Then there was darkness again, followed by a clap of thunder so monstrous that it was as though the earth had split in two.

"What is it?" John asked when he could speak.

"Nothing, I – I thought I saw him – over there."

Another flash of lightning lit up the space.

It was empty.

"Rena, you're getting him on the brain. You were the one who said we shouldn't do that."

"Yes It must have been my imagination," she said, dazed. "Of course."

"Come along."

He grasped her arm and guided her firmly away. In a few minutes they were out of the wood, battling across the open space to the sanctuary of the house.

Never had the kitchen seemed so welcoming. They

slammed the door behind them, drew the curtains and huddled over the range, which still had some warmth.

"Tea," she said, filling the kettle.

"My poor girl! Are you all right? It's not like you to have hallucinations."

"I know, but I think you're right. I'm letting my mind dwell on him, and I mustn't. Oh John, what did we find? Do look."

He took out the coin which he had thrust into his pocket, then felt around in the purse and took out another one. They were the same as the others.

"They might be so valuable that these few are enough," he said hopefully.

But they both knew it was a forlorn hope.

"How do we find out?" she asked.

"I told you I came back from the tavern the other night to write letters. One was to an old friend in London. He's a retired clergyman, and also a very learned historian, with a great knowledge of antiques. I met him when I was a young midshipman in the Navy."

John reddened before he added, "He got me out of a bit of trouble. All my own fault."

"I'm sure you were a demon," Rena laughed.

He nodded. "I wasn't the best behaved lad in the world. Anyway, I wrote to the Reverend Adolphus Tandy. I described the coins as well as I could, hoping that he might write back to tell me what they were. We shall just have to wait for his reply."

He was drowned out again by a violent crack of thunder overhead, followed by the sound of rain pounding down.

There seemed nothing for it but to go to bed and hope for better weather in the morning.

Rena woke to a drenched world. During the night the rain had flattened the long grass and swollen the stream. She slipped outside and breathed in the cool, clean air.

She had meant to go straight in again, but something drew her down to the bridge. On this bright morning the fears of the night before seemed absurd.

She stood on the bridge looking down into the racing water, enjoying the beauty of the day. Of course she hadn't really seen Mr. Wyngate in the flash of lightning. He was just an ordinary man, and could be fought, like any other man.

So lost was she in these thoughts that she did not hear the approach of footsteps, and it was something in the silence that made her look up.

And she saw him.

He was standing just a few feet away, watching her in silence.

The shock was terrible.

It was as though a demon had come up through a trapdoor. Rena had no idea how long he had been there, his cold, dead eyes fixed upon her.

"Good morning," she said, trying to sound firm.

He didn't bother with courtesies.

"You're a very clever woman," he grated. "Cleverer than I thought at first. Only a really sharp intelligence can play the idiot as well as you did."

"You flatter me, sir. I assure you it was no performance."

"Don't waste my time with that stuff," he snapped. "We both know what this is about."

"Then you have the advantage of me."

He sighed impatiently. "I thought better of your wits

than this."

"Shall we go into the house and I can inform His Lordship – ?"

"Stay where you are. It's you I came to see. Walk with me."

He left the bridge and began to follow the rough path to the trees. Rena followed him.

"I thought you had returned to London," she ventured to say.

"I put up at the local hotel last night," he said tersely. "There are things to be said."

"Then let me call the Earl –"

"Not to him, to you," he interrupted her. "Just wait until I'm ready."

Suddenly he stopped and swung round, staring at the house. They were now some distance from it and had a clear view of the whole structure, with the tower rising incongruously but magnificently from the centre.

"The man who built that house knew what he was doing when he added the tower," Wyngate said abruptly.

"The tower isn't part of the original structure," Rena pointed out. "It was added a hundred years later by the seventh Earl."

"Then he knew what he was doing. A man could climb up to the top of that and be monarch of all he surveys. That's what a tower is for. It should be bigger. Much bigger."

"It's already too large for the house," Rena objected.

"It should be bigger," Wyngate said obstinately.

An uneasy feeling was creeping over her. They had seen this man off the day before, and now he was back as though nothing had happened. Had his mind actually taken in the fact that John had refused? She began to think it hadn't.

Wyngate's gaze was still fixed on the tower. He spoke to Rena without looking at her.

"The trouble with my daughter is that she never seems to be interested in the men I want her to be interested in."

"Maybe that's because you can't choose for another person," Rena replied. "It's up to her and I think it would be foolish of her to marry someone unless she was very much in love with him."

Her voice unconsciously softened on the last words. She felt as though a dream had come over her, but she was startled out of it by his furious voice.

"Matilda will love and marry the man I want her to. What woman is capable of choosing well, when her father is as rich as I am?

"Of course men will want to marry her because they know I am rattling with golden sovereigns, but I know what is best."

"Then it seems to me that your money is her misfortune," Rena replied quietly.

"Rubbish! Don't talk in that drivelling fashion. I know who will make her happy, not only for a short time, but for the rest of her life. That is why she must learn to obey me!"

"You care nothing for her happiness but only for your own.," Rena said. "You think only of trying to make yourself bigger and more important than you really are."

"What did you say?"

Her temper was beginning to rise. "You heard exactly what I said. Love comes from the heart and only God can bestow it."

At last he withdrew his gaze from the house, and turned to stare at her.

"Are you serious?" he asked. "Are you saying that love is something religious?"

"Of course it is," Rena replied. "People search for it, hoping that if they can't find it in this life, they will do so in the world to come."

"Stuff and nonsense! Marriage is what women are there for and to produce children who will carry on the name and position of their father."

"That is what you think," Rena retorted. "I believe that love comes from God. When we fall in love it is something holy and it mustn't be thrown aside by money, position or anything which is of importance in this world."

He stared at her as though unable to believe his ears.

"I think you really believe all that stuff."

"Passionately!"

He gave a grunt that might almost have been humorous.

"Well, maybe you think you do. You'll change your tune when you hear what I have to say."

"Mr. Wyngate, I am not interested in anything you have to say."

"Everyone is interested in money, Mrs. Colwell. Or should I say, Miss Colwell?"

If he had hoped to disconcert her he was disappointed. To his astonishment Rena laughed.

"Miss is correct. My father was the vicar here until recently, now I'm Lord Lansdale's housekeeper. He invented a husband for me to prevent you thinking exactly what you are thinking."

"You're very frank."

"Ah, but I don't care in the least what you think of me, Mr. Wyngate." She could hardly believe that it was herself who had said those words. Was she really this cool, composed female who challenged this unpleasant man, and refused to let him disconcert her?

It was he who backed down, pretending not to hear her last remark.

"So your father was a clergyman. They always think that God will turn up at the last moment and do for them what they should have done for themselves a long time ago. But people who want money, have to fight for it."

"And what about the people who don't want money, Mr. Wyngate?"

"They don't exist," he said savagely.

"They exist, but in a world you can't enter." She added softly, "That's why you hate them."

He swung round on her and the malevolence was there in his eyes again. She had flicked him on the raw this time.

"I don't hate them," he said at last. "I despise them. Once you have money you can buy many things which make a human being happy."

"Yes," she said unexpectedly. "Many things. But not all. Your tragedy is that you don't know the difference."

"What do you mean, tragedy?"

"The greatest tragedy in the world."

"Don't feel sorry for me!" he screamed.

She didn't answer.

"Don't feel sorry for me," he repeated emphatically.

"It's time I was going in."

"Wait! I haven't said what I came to say to you. I recognise you as a formidable woman. I respect that."

She was silent.

"Name your price," he said at last.

"Please stand aside and let me pass. I have work to do."

"I said name your price. You can make it a high one. You're an obstacle in my way, and I'm prepared to remove you in a way that's pleasant to yourself. You get out of here and you can have a comfortable life on my money."

"You don't really think you can bribe me?" she demanded. "You must have taken leave of your senses."

"Look, there's no need for outraged virtue. I've said I'll pay you well, so don't waste my time with meaningless mouthings."

Rena regarded him curiously, as she might have studied a loathsome insect.

"You'll – pay – well?" she mused.

"Extremely well."

"That sounds splendid, but it isn't very specific."

"So you want figures. Five thousand pounds."

She laughed.

"Very well, ten thousand!"

"I thought you were a serious man, Mr. Wyngate. Good day to you."

She tried to move past him but he grasped her arm and snapped, "If I go higher than that I'll want more than your silence in return. Is that what you're after, you grasping little doxy?"

Before she could answer this insult he said something that took her breath away.

"Very well, you can have it. I'll set you up in a fine house in Park Lane. You can have jewels, servants, cash, a box at the opera, all the clothes you want. And you'll belong to me, any hour of the day or night that it pleases me."

He meant it, she thought, her mind reeling. She had a wild desire to laugh. A moment ago she had felt insulted, but this was too monstrous for that.

And then came the wicked thought –

"I must share this joke with John. How we'll laugh together!"

She pulled herself together. Her own reprehensible

amusement was surely the most shocking thing of all.

"There is no point in discussing this further," she said. "I'm going now."

"You'll discuss it as long as I want," he shouted, tightening his hand on her arm.

"There is nothing to say," she shouted back. "You do not appeal to me, sir. Is that plain enough for you?"

"Don't tell me my money doesn't appeal to you. What'll happen if you stay here? A drudge all your life, ending up destitute? You don't think he'll marry you, do you?"

She froze, meeting his eyes in horrified self-discovery.

How had this cruel demon put his finger on a secret buried so deep that she hadn't even seen it herself until now?

"All this fancy talk about love," Wyngate sneered. "Weaving pretty dreams for yourself, aren't you? Dreams and nothing else. His mistress is all you'll ever be. He needs money and you don't have it.

"Well, if you can be his mistress, you can be mine, and I'll give you a better time than he could. I know how to treat a woman, you see – in bed and out of it."

"Until you throw her out and she's just as destitute as before," Rena snapped.

"Then you'll have to keep me happy so that I don't, won't you? By God, I'm going to enjoy owning you! What a fight of it we'll have, my lady. I'll enjoy that. I'll overcome you in the end, but it'll be a pleasure showing you who's the master. You're a worthy opponent, you see, and I haven't had one of those for a long time."

Disgust had silenced her, but now she found her tongue.

"Let go of me at once," she said breathlessly. "I will not be your mistress, now or ever. I will not accept your money on any pretext, and I will not be driven out."

"Then we will be enemies," he said coldly. "People who make an enemy of me always regret it. For your own sake, don't be my enemy, Miss Colwell."

She met his eyes, refusing to back down.

"I have been your enemy since the moment I saw you," she said with calm deliberation, "and I shall be your enemy until the moment of my death."

"Which may be sooner than you think, if you continue to be so unwise."

"Don't try to frighten me –" she began.

And then she screamed.

For she had seen two of him.

Another Wyngate had appeared behind him, standing quietly, watching them.

In her overwrought state the sight terrified her as nothing else could have done.

"Shut up, damn you!" Wyngate raged.

For answer she pointed over his shoulder, screaming again and again. Wyngate turned to follow her finger, and then he grew very still, and his grasp on her relaxed enough for her to escape.

She ran for her life. The terrible sight seemed to have drained all the strength from her body, so that each step was an effort, but she kept going.

A turn in the road gave her the chance to look back, and what she saw increased her horror.

The two Wyngates were walking towards each other.

She knew now what was going to happen. When these demons met they would merge into one. And if she saw it happen she would be damned.

She turned away and ran on, desperately, stumbling, falling, gasping, sobbing, desperate to reach the safety of the house, and John.

"John," she cried. "John!"

And then, as though by some blessed miracle, he appeared through the French windows.

"Rena, what on earth – ? My poor girl, what is it?"

It was a blessed mercy to feel his strong, human arms about her, hear his down to earth voice that seemed to have the power to drive out that other, fearful world that had seemed to threaten her.

"Wyngate," she gasped, "he was here."

"He dared to come back?"

"Yes – he was in the grounds – he talked to me – such terrible things – but then – John, there were two of him."

"I don't understand."

"He was there twice. I was talking to him and then he appeared again behind himself."

"Rena –"

"No, no, I'm not mad. I saw it. There were two of him, and I screamed so hard that he let me go, and I ran away. And when I looked back they were walking towards each other."

"Where was this?"

"Just past the bridge. You can see them from here."

He looked over her head, and a slight frown came over his face. Then he walked forward to a place where he could get a better view, showing the land sweeping down to the stream, and beyond it the trees.

Rena came to stand beside him, and then she felt the hairs begin to stand up on the back of her neck.

There was nobody there.

CHAPTER SEVEN

"Are you sure you haven't been raiding the wine cellar?" John asked solicitously, as they went back inside. "You're very welcome, but it may not be doing you much good – no, no of course not," he amended hastily, meeting her fulminating eye.

"John, I know what I saw."

"You saw two copies of Wyngate, who merged into each other, and then vanished into thin air."

"I didn't actually see them merge. I just knew they were going to."

He looked at her.

"All right, I know what I sound like."

"You sound like someone who's been under too much strain, and needs to have somebody else cook breakfast for her," he said, shepherding her into the kitchen. "Now sit down. Clara has outdone herself this morning. Two beautiful eggs. What are you doing?" She was moving towards the kettle.

"It's my job to make the breakfast."

"And I've said I'm doing it, so sit down."

"But – "

"Sit!" he finished sternly, standing over her and wagging an admonitory finger.

"Yes John," she said meekly.

How dear this practical man was, and how easily he could drive her fears away with his kindly common sense.

And oh, how much she loved him!

It had been there, waiting to spring out and surprise her all the time. Then Wyngate had thrust it brutally into the light, forcing her to face what otherwise she might have tried not to see.

For how could she love him? What future could they have, when he didn't love her, and knew his duty to his neighbours?

Those neighbours had always been her friends, kindly people who trusted her to do her best for them, as they had trusted her father. They had nursed her when she was ill, given to her out of their own poverty and refused to take a penny in return.

Now they needed something back from her.

It mustn't be Wyngate's daughter. She was more resolved on that than ever. But there were other heiresses. An Earl would have no trouble attracting them, especially if he was young and handsome with laughing eyes, a sweet temper and a kind heart. And in one of them he would find the woman he could truly love. That was as it should be.

"Here you are, my lady," he said, serving up. While she had been lost in her dream he had made breakfast.

She smiled at him, discovering that it was possible to be happy and sad at the same time. The sadness was for the impossibility of making a life with him, but greater, far greater, was the happiness that swamped her as she contemplated him.

She had only known for a few minutes that she loved him, but already he looked different, more vivid, more intense. How could she ever have thought of him as a brother?

She had discovered the greatest joy known to a

woman, that of knowing that she had given her love to a man who was in every way worthy of love.

"Now tell me what happened out there," he said, pouring her tea.

The tea was delicious, and so was the egg that he had boiled her. Forget the bleak future. It was enough just to be here with him.

"I stepped out for a breath of fresh air, and went down to the bridge. And he just appeared beside me."

"You mean he sprang up out of nowhere?" John asked, his eyes twinkling.

"No, he must have walked across the grass, but I didn't see him."

"He was invisible?"

Her lips twitched. "No, I was looking down into the water."

"How long?"

"I don't know. I was thinking."

"So he had time to walk across the grass?"

She sighed. "Yes, he must have."

"But where did he come from? I thought they went back to London."

"No, they put up at a hotel nearby. He hasn't given up. And this means, of course, that I did see him in the wood last night. He must have come back to spy, and seen the lamp."

"Why didn't you bring him into the house?"

"It wasn't you he wanted to see. He had something to say to me."

"What?"

"He offered me a bribe. He's convinced that if I shut up and got out he could get you into his trap. So he tried to buy me for five thousand pounds."

"The devil he did!" He was eyeing her, fascinated.

"What did you say to him?"

"I pushed him up to ten thousand."

"You what? Rena, you don't mean you – ?"

"Of course not. Don't be absurd. I'd hardly be sitting here telling you about it if I was going to take his money. No, I just wanted to see how high I could push him – just for curiosity."

"And how much is your compliance worth to him?"

"Ten thousand. I can't tell you how delightful it felt to turn him down. I don't think anyone's done that for years. Oh, my goodness!"

She straightened up suddenly, her hands over her mouth as a shattering thought occurred to her.

"Rena, what is it?"

"I shouldn't have turned him down. I should have taken the ten thousand and given it to you. Oh, how could I be so stupid?"

"Cheat him, you mean?" John asked, grinning.

"After all the people he must have cheated by now, it's about time somebody did it to him."

Sweet heaven! Papa would have a fit.

With his uncanny ability to read her mind, John asked, "Is this the kind of thinking you learned at the parsonage?"

"No, I invented it myself," she said defiantly. "Papa would be shocked."

"And very surprised I should think."

"No, not surprised. He always said the tone of my mind left room for improvement."

"I think the tone of your mind is perfect. It's very sweet of you to want to do this for me, but don't blame yourself for not thinking of it in time. I doubt you could really have fooled him. He wouldn't have given you a penny until you were well away from here and it was too late."

Rena nodded. "You're right. He's just the sort of mean, suspicious character who'd do that."

"So what happened when you'd turned him down? How did he react to your refusal."

She shrugged, unwilling to tell him more.

"Rena, what is it? Did he dare to attack you?"

"No, of course not."

"Then what? Please don't keep things from me. Rena! For pity's sake, you're scaring me."

"He wanted to buy me in another way," she said, not looking at him.

"You mean he – ?"

She shrugged and said as lightly as she could, "He offered to set me up in a fine house in Park Lane, clothes, jewels, everything I could want."

"He did what?" The words came from him in a violent whisper.

"I turned that down too and he became very angry."

"He dared say such a thing to you?" John asked quietly. "He dared to besmirch you, even in his thoughts?" He got abruptly to his feet.

"John, where are you going?"

"To find him and throttle him."

There was a black look on his face that she had never seen before. Suddenly the amiable joker she knew had vanished, replaced by a man in a bitter rage.

"No." She jumped to her feet and followed him out of the kitchen. "You mustn't do that."

"You expect me to do nothing, when he insults you?" He started up the stairs.

"Where are you going?"

"To get my pistol."

She began to run after him up the stairs, struggling to

keep up. He had reached his room before she caught him.

"John, listen to me, there's nothing that you can do."

"I can make him sorry he was born. I can bring him here and make him grovel to you – "

"And how much reputation would I have left then?" She took hold of his arms and gave him a little shake. She could feel him trembling with rage.

"Then I'll blow his miserable brains out," he shouted. "Yes, that's the thing to do. Then the filthy thoughts that he dared to have of you will be blown to smithereens, and nobody will ever know that he insulted the sweetest, most perfect woman alive. Rena, Rena, do you expect me to endure that?"

She didn't know how to answer such words, but she didn't have to because the next moment he had pulled her into his arms and was kissing her fiercely again and again, murmuring incoherently between kisses.

"You're mine – do you understand? I won't tolerate that man even looking at you, much less thinking – Dear God! Kiss me, my darling – kiss me –tell me that it isn't all in my mind – say that you love me too – "

"Oh yes – yes – I love you, so much."

She had promised herself that she would never tell him of her love, for his sake. And yet the words burst from her, called forth by the intensity of his own emotion. He loved her. He had said so. And nothing in heaven or on earth could have prevented her from confessing her own love in return.

"I love you," he said, holding her away from him so that he could see her face. "I love you in every way that a man can love a woman. You are mine, and I am yours. That is how it has to be. It was meant. It's our destiny. I couldn't fight it if I wanted to. But I don't. I want to love you and rejoice in you all the days of my life. And if you don't feel the same I have nothing to live for."

"But I do," she cried. "I do. Oh John – my love – "

"Kiss me," he said again, and this time it was a command.

She obeyed it gladly. The future might contain a bitter parting, but in this moment she would enjoy her love to the full. The bliss of being chosen by the one her own heart had chosen was too sweet to be denied.

"Tell me again that you love me," he said. "Let me hear you say it."

"I love you, I love you," she murmured. "I didn't think love could happen this fast – I never knew – "

"It can happen in a moment," he said fervently. "I loved you the first day. Didn't you feel then that our hearts instinctively understood each other?"

"Oh yes, yes. I felt that too, even though we were strangers."

"We were never strangers," he told her tenderly. "We have known each other for ever, and we shall be each other's until the last moment of our lives."

"Until the last moment of our lives," she agreed solemnly.

She didn't voice her fears for their future. Besides, it was true. Even though life might separate them, she would always belong to him. After this, there could be no other man.

"How could I marry any woman but you?" he asked lovingly.

"John – "

She was saved from having to answer by the sound of the doorbell, echoing up from below.

"If that's Wyngate – " he said in a tight voice.

"No, John, please. You must pretend to know nothing, for my sake."

"We'll see," was all he would agree to.

Together they went downstairs to open the front door.

But the man standing there wasn't Wyngate. Neither of them had seen him before. He was tall and thin, dressed in clerical black, with a severe face and stern eyes.

"Miss Colwell?" he asked at once.

"Yes."

He spoke ponderously. "I am the Reverend Steven Daykers. I imagine you have been expecting me."

It would have been impolite to say otherwise, so Rena murmured something about being honoured to meet him. She hastened to introduce the Earl, but instead of being pleased the Reverend Daykers fixed him with a frosty stare, and gave him the briefest of greetings.

"Miss Colwell, a word with you alone." It was a command.

John looked at her, frowning. Maintaining an air of calm dignity Rena said, "If I may have a few moments from my duties, sir?"

He caught the cue she had tossed him. "Very well Miss Colwell, I suggest you use the drawing room. But please try not to be too long."

"What I have to say to Miss Colwell will not take a moment," the pastor said with a touch of grimness.

Rena led him to the drawing room and politely offered him tea. He waved the suggestion aside.

"I have not come for trifles, but for your salvation. You visited my house the other evening – "

"I wasn't aware that it was your house, since the letter informing me did not arrive until the following morning. As soon as I learned the situation I packed my things and departed."

"There was, I believe, some altercation between you

and my sister concerning certain property – "

"They wanted to eat my chicken for supper. Since she belongs to me I would not permit that."

"You referred to my house as a den of thieves!"

"They were trying to deprive me of my property," Rena said firmly. "I don't have very much. I insist on my right to protect what I have."

Unexpectedly he nodded.

"Precisely so. I understand that you are not well endowed with this world's goods, and therefore you may have felt yourself impelled into this – ah – disgraceful situation."

"I beg your pardon!"

"It is well known, Miss Colwell, that you, an unmarried woman, share this house with the Earl, an unmarried man, with no respectable female companion."

"I am his lordship's housekeeper," Rena said, her eyes sparkling with anger. "A servant. Servants do not have 'respectable female companions'. They have to take the work that will put a roof over their heads."

"I have already said that I understand that you were constrained by circumstances. Nor is it my intention to apportion blame to one who has erred in – I feel sure – innocence. I am here to rescue you."

"But I do not need rescue."

"Madam, your need for rescue is greater than you can possibly know. A young woman's reputation, beautiful and fragile as it is, must call forth all the protective instincts of those whose mission in life is to protect lost souls. You have strayed – yes. Sadly that is true. But you have not wandered far from the path, and there is yet time to turn you back."

Rena stared at him, scarcely able to believe what she was hearing.

"I believe – I fervently believe that your stay in this

101

house has not yet compromised your virtue though it has endangered your reputation. If you escape at once all is not lost. I shall take you back with me to the vicarage where you may embark upon that path of righteousness that will in time undo the harm."

"I'm not going back there," Rena said, aghast. "And I feel sure that your sister doesn't want me."

"On the contrary, she is eager for your return. Her last words to me were not to come back without you. There are many ways in which you can make yourself useful in that house which you know better than anyone. Her health is not strong – "

"And she would like to have an unpaid drudge around," Rena said, light dawning.

"Young woman, I am not here to bandy words with you, but to take you home."

"The parsonage is no longer my home. Now I think you should leave."

"You dare to show me an impudent spirit! I have come to offer you my protection. Your father was a brother man of the cloth, and now I stand in his place. I demand from you the obedience of a daughter."

"No sir, you do not stand in my father's place. He was the best and kindest man who ever lived, and he would never have tried to bully anyone in the way you have me. I owe you no obedience and will give you none."

"I say, Miss Colwell – sorry to butt in and all that – but have you seen my cigars?"

John had entered by the French windows and now stood on the threshold, smiling amiably but implacably.

"Hallo, vicar. You still here? Hope you've finished your little talk because my housekeeper has a great deal of work to get on with. Come now, Miss Colwell, be about your duties. Mustn't fall behind, must we?"

"I do not consider this a suitable position for Miss Colwell," the vicar said stiffly.

"Oh no, no, no!" John said, still amiable, but standing between them in a manner that couldn't be mistaken. "She does her job very well. Couldn't do without her. Shall I show you to the door?"

The Reverend Daykers had no choice but to follow his host, but he had one parting shot for Rena.

"I shall not cease in my untiring efforts to reclaim you."

When he had gone Rena sat down, not sure whether to laugh or cry. The man was a pompous fool who deceived himself as to his own motives, yet he had shown her how the world would view her, a world in which she would soon have to make her way alone again.

John was in a merry mood when he returned.

"I'm afraid I eavesdropped shamelessly outside the French windows," he said, dropping down on the sofa beside her, and taking her hands in his.

"I'm glad you did. He was getting difficult to handle. As though I'd go back and drudge for that family."

"As though I'd let you. And who cares what people say? We'll be married soon."

"John, please don't be so certain of that. I'm not sure we can ever be married."

"Why, what are you talking about? Of course we're going to be married, now that we know we love each other. That's what people in love do, my darling. They marry each other."

"And the people who are depending on you as their last hope? Do we just turn our backs and leave them to starve?"

He stared at her, aghast as it dawned on him that she was serious.

"Are you saying we have no right think of our own

happiness?" he asked at last.

"Perhaps we don't." She jumped up from the sofa and moved away from him, as though by doing so she could break the spell that bound her to him.

But he followed her at once, taking hold of her and drawing her round to face him.

"I won't accept that. We love each other – " his face was suddenly full of fear, "Rena, you do love me? You said so. Let me hear you say it again."

"Of course I love you, with all my heart. It's been such a short time, and yet already you're my whole world. John my darling, don't ever doubt my love for you."

He relaxed a little, but held her against him as though afraid that some power might snatch her away.

"You must never talk like this again," he said. "I've sailed the world, always looking for my ideal woman, in country after country. And at last I found her here, my perfect treasure. Do you think I'm going to let that treasure go? Rena, my darling – "

His lips were on hers again in a kiss that blotted out all argument. Rena gave herself up to her happiness, glorying in his love, knowing that stern reality had to be faced soon but – not yet – not yet –

When he released her she took his face between her hands and looked at him fervently.

"I shall love you," she said, "all my life, and beyond. Never forget that."

Her beautiful soul was in her eyes. He saw it and took her hand, kissing it with reverence.

"Then we shall always be together," he said. "Give me your promise."

"John, I – "

"Give it to me," he insisted.

How could she give him such a promise, she thought wildly, knowing that she might have to break it? Yet how could she break so solemn a vow to the man she loved?

Her duty seemed clear to her. Let him go for the sake of those who looked to him for succour. She averted her eyes from that duty, lest her heart break, but when she opened them it was still there.

Matilda had said, "I'm not Jeremiah Wyngate's daughter for nothing."

She, Rena, was not the Reverend Colwell's daughter for nothing. Much of his teaching might have fallen away from her recently, but not that: not the obligation to put others' needs first, at whatever cost to oneself.

"Rena – promise me that we will be married," he said, speaking in a stern voice that she had never heard him use before.

"I – "

But before she could answer a shadow appeared in the open French windows and a strong, female voice cried,

"Thank heavens I've found you. You simply must help us."

It was Matilda, and behind her was a young man with red hair and a plain, freckled face.

"This is Cecil Jenkins," she said. "I told you about him."

This was the man she loved, and by the note in her voice Rena knew of her pride and joy.

"Cecil?" John asked.

"I promised Matilda I would keep her secret," Rena explained. "She and Cecil are in love."

"And we want to marry," the young man said. "It's just that Mr. Wyngate is the problem."

"This is wonderful," John exclaimed. "At least he'll

stop trying to dragoon me into being his son-in-law."

"If you think that, you don't know my father," Matilda said. "Cecil had to come here in secret and hide in the bushes in the hotel garden until I came out. Now we desperately need your help. If Papa discovers that he's here he'll be furious. He's so set on having Lord Lansdale as a son-in-law."

"I don't think you should say that in front of Cecil," John objected mildly.

"Cecil knows that I love him," Matilda said passionately, "and I wouldn't have you at any price – no offence intended."

"None taken," John said affably. "I feel the same – no offence intended."

"Of course. You're in love with Rena, aren't you? I told her you were, but she wouldn't believe me. But after what I've just seen I know it's true. I wish you both every happiness. But it doesn't mean that Papa has given up."

"He's bringing men up here to move into the house," Cecil said. "Thirty of them."

John and Rena looked at each other, appalled.

"But how could you possibly know that?" John demanded.

"I know the firm of architects that he's employing," Cecil said. "The head man is a friend of mine. Mr. Wyngate gave his orders last week – "

"Last week?" John exclaimed. "Before he came here?"

"That's how Papa works," Matilda explained. "First he lays his plans, then he investigates to see if there'll be any opposition."

"And if there is, he deals with it," Cecil said. "They're only waiting for his message to move in here."

"And when they arrive," Matilda cried, "you won't be

106

able to stop them, because when people take their orders from Papa they're too scared of him to disobey."

"But this is my house," John said.

"That won't make any difference. They're not scared of you, they're scared of him."

Matilda's voice rose to a note of hysteria.

"You think you can fight him, but you can't. Nobody can fight Papa. We might as well give in now."

CHAPTER EIGHT

Cecil took Matilda into his arms, soothing her after her hysterical outburst. When she had finished sobbing she managed a smile and wiped her eyes.

"Sometimes I can't help doing that," she explained shakily. "I mean to be strong and brave, but then I remember how powerful he is, and how he can be everywhere at once."

"Please ma'am, don't talk like that," John begged. "You sound like Rena. According to her he divided himself into two this morning, then merged back and vanished."

"John, that's most unfair," Rena protested. "It was an illusion, because I was upset."

"But what did you see?" Matilda asked, wide-eyed.

Rena again described the incident, but this time leaving out the part where Wyngate had tried to make her his mistress. And she tried to make light of the 'appearance' of his double.

But it was no use. Matilda's eyes were wide with horror.

"You've seen it too?" she whispered. "And so have I."

"Matilda, my dear," Cecil chided her lovingly. "That cannot be."

"But it can. It's how Papa spies on people. When I was a little girl, in the park with my governess he used to divide himself and appear, although I knew we'd just left him

108

at home. He would stand there watching me, and then disappear."

"Did your governess see him?" Rena asked.

"No, she always said I was imagining things."

"Did you tell your father?" Rena asked.

Matilda solemnly shook her head. "I was too scared. He must be very determined if he's started doing this again."

"For the love of heaven, both of you," John said in alarm, "you talk as though this fantasy was real, but it can't be. There simply has to be a rational explanation." He scratched his head. "I only wish I could think what it was."

"We're probably both so un-nerved by him that we've started hallucinating," Rena said, with an attempt at cheerfulness.

"But that wouldn't explain why we hallucinate the same thing," Matilda pointed out. "It must be real."

"Then there is a common sense explanation," John said firmly. "In the mean time we have to stop frightening ourselves.

"Of course," Cecil said bravely.

"Yes." Matilda gave herself a little shake, as though pulling herself together by main force. "We will not be beaten."

"We're going to find a way to be together," Cecil promised her. He looked up at the other two. "But we badly need your help."

"You promised you'd help me," Matilda reminded Rena.

"And I will. But what do you want me to do?"

"Let Cecil hide here. He has nowhere else, and Papa mustn't see him. I must hurry back to the hotel before he finds me missing. He thinks I'm lying down."

"Of course he may stay here," John said at once. "But

what is your plan?"

Cecil looked helpless. "While I'm here, I'll see as much of Matilda as possible and – something may happen," he said.

John, the man of action, refrained from giving his frank opinion of this as a strategy, contenting himself with saying mildly, "Perhaps something would be more likely to happen if you gave it some assistance."

"Yes," said Cecil at once. "But how?"

"Please don't fight with Papa," Matilda pleaded with John.

"Tell him not to fight with me," John said at once.

"I mean, when he turns up here, don't send him away. Let him come in and look round as if you were prepared to consider his ideas."

"You mean let him think I'm in the market for his daughter?" John demanded bluntly. "How will that help you?"

"Because if you throw him out he may drag me back to London, and it's much harder for Cecil and me to meet. But when he comes here I can come with him, and then I shall be able to see Cecil."

John looked helplessly at them and from them to Rena.

"I don't like this idea," he said, "but I can't think of a better."

Rena also was uneasy, but she could see no way of refusing. And the more the bonds between Matilda and Cecil were cemented the easier it would be to thwart Wyngate.

"Please come with me," she said to Cecil, "and I will find you a room."

He followed her upstairs and she put him in the room near John's, where it would be easy to keep him under observation.

"You probably think I'm just after Matilda's money," the young man said. "But I do assure you that I'm not. She's such a wonderful girl."

He was a very plain young man, and some girls would have found him uninteresting. But when Rena saw the love light shining from his eyes as he spoke of his beloved she could see exactly what the lonely Matilda found in him to love.

"No, I promise you I don't think that," she assured him kindly. "Besides, I think you know by now that you probably won't get his money."

"Oh I do hope not," he said earnestly. "That would be much better. Of course I want Matilda to have a comfortable life, but I can support her, and she swears to me that she doesn't care about luxury."

He gave a self deprecating laugh.

"You probably think it's naïve of me, to believe her. Easy to say you don't care for luxury when you're surrounded by it. She might feel different later. But I don't think so. She's never had anybody who loved her. Her father only cares about making use of her. But I love her, and she knows it."

"I believe you. How did you two meet?"

"I'm an architect. Mr. Wyngate wanted his own house in London transformed – bigger, grander, more luxurious –"

"I can imagine."

"She was there – the sweetest girl alive – and we talked, and talked. And we fell in love. We planned our future together – I was doing well in the firm, there was a chance of a partnership."

He sighed. "But then he found us together, and the sky descended on us. I have never seen a man so lividly angry. He had me thrown out of the house bodily, there and then, and locked Matilda in her room for a week.

"He demanded that she promise never to see me again. When she refused I was waylaid on a street corner by thugs, and beaten until I nearly died."

"Sweet heaven!" Rena murmured, appalled.

"I was taken to hospital and she was brought to see me there so that she could witness the results of her 'disobedience'."

Rena buried her face in her hands.

"She gave him that promise," Cecil said. Then he looked at her closely. "Matilda says you're a parson's daughter, Miss Colwell."

She raised her head. "That's right," she said huskily.

"Will it shock you very much if I say that neither Matilda nor myself had the slightest intention of keeping such a promise?"

"Not in the slightest" Rena said in a decisive tone. "In my opinion nobody should feel bound by a promise extracted in such a way."

"Then you do not blame us?"

"I think you should get her away from him as soon as possible, and go to a place where he can't find you."

She spoke impulsively and his wry look showed that he knew it.

Some place where Wyngate's arm could not reach.

Was there such a place?

As if to confirm her thoughts, Cecil added,

"I said I was doing well in the firm, but since then I haven't been able to get work. Wyngate's influence stretches far, and everyone is afraid of him."

"Oh how angry I get when I hear that!" Rena flashed. "Everyone is afraid of Wyngate! We must not be afraid of him."

She finished dusting, glad of a prosaic occupation to

set against the horrors in her mind.

"Let us go down now," she said, "and you can look for some books in the library to while away the long hours I'm afraid you will have to spend up here. After what you've told me it's more than ever vital to keep you hidden."

They began to head back the way they had come. But at the top of the stairs they heard a voice that made them both start back and flatten themselves against the wall.

"It's him," Cecil said. "Mr. Wyngate."

The man's hated voice seemed to combine the cawing of a rook with the sound of a coin scratching across glass. It reached them clearly up the stairs.

"Get back to your room quickly," she murmured.

She gave him a moment to get out of sight, then descended, hoping against hope that John had not reacted badly to the sight of Wyngate, but was playing his part successfully.

She forced herself to be composed as she entered the drawing room to find Wyngate there, standing between Matilda and John, a hand on the shoulder of each.

"I was a little disturbed when I found my dear one wasn't in her room, as I expected her to be," he said, with a ghastly smile at his daughter. "But then I realised where she must have gone, and so I came to find her, and here she is. You couldn't keep away, could you, my pet?"

"It's such a beautiful house, Papa," Matilda said woodenly.

"Indeed it is. And it will be better still when I've spent some money on it."

Even from across the room Rena could sense John's struggle to keep his composure. He was doing his best to stay calm, but he moved away from Wyngate's hand and said firmly,

"That still remains to be seen. I'm by no means sure

that I can accept your help, sir, and I advise you against any precipitate moves."

"Don't you worry, m'boy. I know my own business best."

"I'm sure of it, sir. But it is my business we are discussing," said John in a cool voice.

Wyngate's smiled slipped a little, but only a little. He had succeeded in getting back into the house, which was his main objective. The rest could wait until these fools realised the futility of fighting him. His smile in Rena's direction contained more than a hint of a sneer.

"Why, it's the little housekeeper." He stressed the last word very slightly, as though reminding her that it was her own fault that she was still in this lowly position.

"May I bring you and your guests some refreshment, sir?" she asked John.

"None of that," Wyngate said, not troubling to ask what his daughter would like. "I want to see the tower."

"But you have already seen the tower," Rena said. "This morning – "

"Not like that. I want to go up to the roof and see it close up. I have an idea for its improvement."

"I doubt if it can be improved," John said, keeping his temper.

"Things can always be improved, young man, if it's done in the right way. That tower tells people who you are."

"But I don't need an edifice to tell people who I am," John replied quietly. "I am Lord Lansdale and I am the master here. I am. Nobody else."

At those firm words Wyngate shot him a sharp look as though scenting rebellion. John returned his gaze with a bland one of his own, but his blue eyes were hard.

"Of course you're the master here," Wyngate said at last. "Nobody doubts it. Lord Lansdale, master of his acres.

114

But on my money, eh? Come along, I don't want to waste any more time. You two young people take a walk in the garden together. Your housekeeper can show me up to the tower."

"No, we'll all go," John said. "As the master of the house I prefer to entertain you myself."

Rena knew that nothing on earth would have persuaded him to let her go up there alone with Wyngate.

"Then shall we begin the climb to the roof?" she asked. "It's quite difficult and tiring. And you must be careful where you walk because the roof isn't very safe. It's easy for your foot to go through."

She remembered a long time ago when she had visited this house with Papa, and the old Earl had shown her the tower. Luckily the keys hung in the same place now as then, and she fetched them quickly. A climb of three floors brought them out onto the roof.

It was the best spring day they had had so far, and the four of them stood there in the bright sun, looking at the sunlit land spread out before them.

"How charming," Matilda said. "You can see ever so far."

"Not far enough," Wyngate said. "Higher. I want to see more."

In the centre was the tower itself, a square shape, extending right from the front of the roof to the back, rearing thirty feet above them, with little turrets around the edge. Rena unlocked the door, and John led the way up the stairs, contriving to squeeze her hands reassuringly as he passed her.

After climbing thirty feet they came out into the air, gasping at the gusts of wind that assailed them. Matilda gave a little scream and clutched John. Wyngate would have given his arm to Rena but she declined and held on to the top of one of the turrets. But it immediately gave way, leaving her looking down what seemed like an endless drop to the ground.

As though time had slowed, she was able to watch the loose stone falling to the ground and landing with an almighty crash.

For a moment she was dizzy. The terrifying drop yawned before her like a descent into hell. Then she stepped back sharply, giving a prayer of thanks that nobody had been there to be crushed.

Wyngate hadn't noticed the reactions of anybody else. He was looking around him, up into the sky, then out onto the landscape.

"This is right," he said. "This is as it should be. A great man in a great house, presiding over a great estate, needs a great tower from which to survey his domain."

John tried to deflect it as a joke.

"It hadn't occurred to me that I was a great man," he said wryly.

"You will be when I've finished," Wyngate said. "At any time you can come up here and look out for trespassers."

John gave a wry laugh. "You can't see the whole estate from here. Nothing like it."

"You will have men to guard the place, if you are sensible," Mr. Wyngate remarked. "And they should each carry a gun!"

"No," Rena cried. "You can't shoot people who are just taking a little walk or looking for an escaped dog. And with all these acres, you'll never stop children climbing through the hedges to pick flowers, or watch the squirrels."

"That will stop," Wyngate said sharply: "The locals are subservient to the Squire and they will have to learn to behave themselves. Trespassers will be punished severely."

Horrified, Rena looked towards John who met her

eyes, his expression mirroring her own. But he didn't remonstrate with this unpleasant man. He merely shook his head very slowly, unseen by Mr. Wyngate.

"This must be enlarged," Wyngate declared. "It must be twice the height."

"By all means," John said, "if you want the house to fall down."

"What?" Wyngate glared at him.

"In the Navy I learned that the hull is the most important part of the ship," John continued. "Everything depends on that being strong, and capable of carrying not only the rest of the ship, but everyone on it.

"If you want to enlarge the tower you should strengthen the foundations first. Then work up, strengthen and secure the roof. Then, and only then, can you think about the tower. Otherwise, the increased weight will only bring the whole thing down."

Wyngate glared. He was shrewd enough to recognise that he would look foolish challenging the Earl on this matter, but he still couldn't accept defeat graciously.

"We'll see," he grated. "We'll see. But I insist on twice the height."

"You had much better abandon the whole idea," John said. "A higher tower would be completely out of proportion to the rest of the building. In fact, even the present height is too much. It should have a few feet taken off."

"I – want – it – twice – the – size," Wyngate said slowly and emphatically.

John shrugged.

"Don't you understand?" Wyngate screamed. "You should let everyone around know that you are here, and that you insist on being obeyed."

"But I don't," John said mildly. "And I prefer to be on good terms with my neighbours."

"Neighbours?" Wyngate sneered. "These are your inferiors. Never forget that."

"They are my neighbours," John said stubbornly. "I don't want them to obey me, I want them to like me."

"Like you? Who cares if they like you?"

"I do."

"Their role is to obey and yours to command. You've been a naval officer. You should know about command."

"I shall probably never know as much about command as you do," John observed. "Or perhaps the word I want is bullying?"

"You can call it what you like," Wyngate sneered. "I didn't get where I am by being a milksop. I expect obedience and I get it, or there's trouble."

He swung back to the view that stretched over hills and vales, across streams and woods, almost to the sea.

"All my life I've dreamed of this – standing on a high place and having dominion over all before me."

"I believe the devil had much the same dream," John said.

"Hah! Do you think to scare me by saying that? Do you think I don't know that they call me the devil? Do you think I mind?"

He bellowed the last words into the wind, and for a moment they saw him, arms upraised in defiance of the world. He had forgotten their existence.

"Come," John said, taking each of the ladies by the arm. "He does not need us, and we are safer below."

They withdrew quietly, walking down the stairs and leaving Wyngate there with his dreams of glory. When they came out on the ground they looked up to see him still there, standing against the sky, oblivious to his isolation.

At last he looked down and saw them on the ground,

looking up at him.

"I suppose we look like ants to him," Matilda said. "That is certainly how he thinks of us. And this is how he wants us to think of him – as far above us."

"Let us simply go quietly inside," said John. "And wait for him to descend in his own time."

It took another hour for Wyngate to join them, and then he showed no awkwardness at the way they had deserted him. Probably, Rena reasoned, he thought that 'lesser folk' had simply withdrawn to allow the 'great man' to brood alone.

Certainly his demeanour when she descended supported this view. He seemed exalted.

"Come, my dear," he said to Matilda. "It is time for us to be going."

He was quieter than usual as he led her out to the waiting carriage. He was still absorbed in some inner dream, and it struck the watchers with a chill.

"It's all right, he's gone," John said, slipping an arm around Rena's shoulders.

"Yes," she said heavily. "It's just that while he was up there, looking out over the countryside, I felt as though he was casting a pall of evil over everything that fell under his gaze."

She gave a little shudder.

"I feel that if we went out there now we'd find every tree and bush withered, and every blade of grass turned brown."

"Now you're being fanciful," he chided her gently. "Just the same, I do know what you mean."

"John," she said suddenly, "Can we go back to the cross? Please, I just want to see it. It'll make me feel better."

"Of course we will. And we can take another look at the earth, to see if we missed anything last night. Let's go now, before the light starts to go."

They hurried down the path and across the bridge. The bright day was fading, and a watery sun sliding down the sky as they entered the woods, which now seemed bathed in an eerie light. To Rena's morbid imagination they had a withered look, as though Wyngate's malign influence had indeed blighted them.

She tried to pull herself together, conscious of John's warm, strong hand holding hers. She was being foolish. Any minute now they would reach the cross, and it would cast its usual comfort over her.

"There it is," said John. "But surely – Rena, I couldn't have dug a hole as big as that last night, could I?"

"You didn't do that," she breathed.

As the foot of where the cross had stood was a hole so large that it seemed only a wild animal could have made it. Some creature in a frenzy had gored into the earth, ripping its heart out.

And the cross that had stood proudly in that earth had been ripped out too, and now lay on its side, abandoned, desecrated.

*

"Wyngate went there last night, after we had gone," John agreed. "He saw us digging in that spot, and went to see what we were looking for. If there were any coins left, they're now in his possession."

It was late at night and they were sitting on the oak settle in the kitchen. Cecil had gone to bed, and they were at last alone with their love, and their despair.

"I wish I hadn't agreed to Matilda's plan to seem complacent with Wyngate," John added.

"I don't think it would have made any difference," said Rena with a sigh. "He makes his plans despite us. It's like being strangled."

"Forget him for now, my love. Hold me and let us

120

dream of better things."

She snuggled against him, willing to allow herself these few precious moments of happiness, perhaps to last a lifetime.

But they were disturbed by a knocking on the front door.

"Who can that be, so late?" John demanded.

"I'll see."

"I'm coming to the door with you," he said, rising. "If it's Wyngate or that bullying clergyman, I'll deal with them."

They made their way through the dark house into the hall. Another storm was brewing outside, with the occasional flash of lightning searing through the windows, then vanishing into darkness again.

John drew the bolts back and Rena opened the door wide enough to see who stood on the step outside.

At that moment there was another flash of lightning, illuminating the stranger from behind, turning him into a silhouette.

Her blood froze, and a scream strangled in her throat.

This was the man who, that morning, had mysteriously appeared and even more mysteriously vanished.

It was the second Wyngate.

CHAPTER NINE

For a moment time seemed to stop. Then John's glad cry rang out,

"Adolphus, my dear fellow. How good to see you."

Before Rena's bewildered eyes he wrung the man's hand and drew him into the house.

"I can't believe this," he kept saying. "You're actually here."

"Can't believe I'm here?" the stranger said. "But you wrote to me. I thought you wanted me to come."

"Of course I hoped you'd be able to come, but I didn't dare think it possible, knowing how busy you are. Rena, this is the friend I told you of, the pastor and historian who may know what the coins are. The Reverend Adolphus Tandy. Adolphus, this is Miss Rena Colwell, the lady I am going to marry."

"Well, well, that's delightful news. My dear, I am so pleased to meet you."

"But we have met before, haven't we?" she said, in a dazed voice. "Or at least, I have seen you before."

"Yes, indeed. Early this morning. I'm so sorry that I gave you a fright. Perhaps I could explain later."

"Of course. Please come in and I'll get you something to eat."

Now she could see that he was a very old man indeed,

possibly deep into his eighties. But his movements were still hearty and vigorous, and his eyes were bright and alert.

As she took his coat she noticed something that she had instinctively known would be there: the shoulders that were too broad for his body, the arms that were too long, the slightly ape-like appearance that she had seen in Wyngate.

She knew now.

But she would wait for him to explain everything in his own time.

John drew the old man through to the warmth of the kitchen, and Rena served him some supper. They had wine now, having explored the wine cellar until they found something drinkable.

As he warmed himself by the fire the Reverend Tandy, or Adolphus as John called him, continually watched Rena. She couldn't be sure whether it was because John had said they were to be married, or because of what he had seen that morning. But his gaze was piercing, although kindly.

His scrutiny did not trouble her because she was also studying him. Despite his disconcerting resemblance to Wyngate this man's presence radiated an intense feeling of good, as strong, if not stronger, than Wyngate's of evil. It was as if some powerful force had come into the dimly lit kitchen, illuminating every corner with hope. Rena did not understand it, but it comforted her.

He was as shabby as the kitchen. His clothes must have been at least ten years old, darned repeatedly, worn at the cuffs, threadbare at the sleeves.

Yet his poverty caused him no sorrow. He had the look of a man at peace with life and his own soul. Whatever he had found in his chosen path, it had brought him fulfilment.

Which was incredible if what she believed was true.

Rena went upstairs and found him somewhere to sleep, her mind spinning with the incredible discovery that she had made.

She couldn't quite see how, but she knew that what had just happened was going to change everything.

When she returned downstairs she found the two men with the coins spread out before them on the kitchen table.

"Your description was excellent," the Reverend Tandy informed John, taking out a large magnifying glass and studying a coin closely. "The details made my mouth water. Yes – yes – excellent."

"You mean – you know what they are?" John asked on a note of rising excitement.

"Oh yes, no doubt about it. My goodness, what a find!"

"Are they valuable?" John persisted, and Rena held her breath.

"They might be worth a very great deal, but not if you only have seven. You see, much of their value resides in their historical interest. They are the last gold sovereigns ever struck in the reign of Charles I. Only thirty were ever minted. The story is that they were given to his eldest son when he went into exile."

"Then they must be scattered far and wide," Rena said.

"No, because the young Prince Charles was so loved that none of his supporters would take a penny in return for hiding and protecting him. And so he arrived in France with his thirty sovereigns intact, and swore never to spend them but always keep them together, to remind him that it was his destiny to return as King Charles II.

"Eventually, of course, that's just what he did. Nobody knows what became of them after that. But the King had a good friend, Jonathan Relton, who had helped him survive during his exile. As a reward Relton was granted this estate and the Earldom of Lansdale.

"The king used to visit the family here. One theory

says that he entrusted Lansdale with the keeping of the coins, which had almost a mystical significance for him by that time."

"And these are the coins?" John asked, awed.

"Some of them, I'm sure of it. If you had all thirty the set might be worth – oh, anything up to a hundred thousand pounds."

Neither of them could say a word. With that money – or even half the sum – they were saved, the Grange was saved, and the villagers were saved.

Yet that hope was still a distant dream.

"But even seven must be worth something," John was almost pleading. "If thirty are worth a hundred thousand, then seven must be worth about twenty three."

"I'm afraid not. The value lies in the completeness of the set. Separately each of these coins might be worth about five hundred pounds."

Three and a half thousand pounds. Not nearly enough to do all that needed to be done. The disappointment was severe.

"But we may yet find the others," Adolphus' voice was encouraging.

"No, Wyngate has them," John said despondently. "He saw us digging there last night, and today we found the place turned over. Whatever was there, he's taken."

"May I ask how he comes to be involved in all this?" Adolphus asked in a quiet voice that made Rena look at him.

"He wants me for his daughter," John said bitterly. "He would have preferred a Duke, but I'll do if necessary. He sees my impoverished state, and he is determined to move in, spreading his money irresistibly wherever he goes."

"Ah yes," Adolphus murmured. "That was always his way."

"You know him?" John asked.

It seemed at first as though Adolphus would not answer this. He stared bleakly at the floor, as though crushed by a burden too great for words. But at last he raised his head, and said, as though the words were torn from him,

"He is my son."

John started up in astonishment. "Adolphus, he can't be. Why, the man's as evil as sin – "

"Let him be," Rena said quietly. "It is true."

Adolphus gave her a faint smile. "You knew at once, didn't you?"

"When you appeared this morning, I thought it was his double. You are shaped so alike. It's an unusual shape. And you were so far off I couldn't see details of your face, although your head is like his too."

"Why that's it," said John suddenly. "I've been trying to think who Wyngate reminds me of, and it's you."

Adolphus nodded, "Not in features, so much, although we both have slightly large heads. It's more in the shape of our bodies."

"That's what I saw this morning," said Rena. "And I was so scared of him, and in such a fretful state, that I fancied he had managed to turn himself into two men. That's why I screamed."

"How rude of me to have frightened you, my dear."

"I'm not scared now that I can see you close. But then I had such wild fancies. I began to run to the house, but I looked back to see you walking towards each other. Then you just vanished."

"Rena told me about it," said John, "and I went to see for myself. But there was nobody there."

"I couldn't see how you could have reached the trees so quickly," said Rena.

"Because my son was determined to get me out of sight as fast as he could," Adolphus replied. "He had no idea

126

that I was there until you screamed, and he turned and saw me.

"It is fifteen years since we last saw each other, and longer than that since we spoke. But he knew me, as I knew him. He wasn't pleased. He hates me as much as I – dread him.

"He came up to me, snarling even before he spoke. 'What the devil do you think you're doing here? Have you come to plague me and cast a blight over me?' He didn't wait for my answer, but seized my arm and dragged me to the trees.

"When we were hidden he said, 'Go away from here and don't come back.'"

He fell silent.

"Whatever did you say to him?" Rena asked.

"Nothing. I merely looked at him in silence. He took a step back from me, raised his arm as if to ward me off, and cried, 'Stay away from me. Don't come near.' Then he turned and walked quickly away."

"You're not safe," said John at once. "He will harm you as he has harmed others."

"No, my dear boy," Adolphus said gently. "He will do me no harm. He will rant and rave, but he will never touch me. He fears me too much for that."

"Wyngate fears nobody," said John.

"You are wrong. There is always some force to be feared, something stronger than ourselves."

"I don't understand how such a man can be born of such a father," said John, brooding.

"I too used to wonder about that. Jane, my dear wife, never knew the worst of him. I used to hide it from her.

"Franklin – that is his real name: Franklin Tandy – was our only child, and she adored him. I couldn't bear to see her heart broken and so I covered up his crimes – childish pranks

I called them, although I knew then in my heart that it was much worse.

"He enjoyed hurting helpless creatures. Pulling the wings off insects was nothing to him, he did far worse. I once saw him kill a kitten by breaking its neck, right in front of the child who owned it. Then he laughed at the child's tears." Adolphus sighed. "He was about seven when he did that."

"Thank God his mother died when he was eighteen, before the depths of him had been revealed. He was at her deathbed, sobbing, and within an hour of her death he had sold her favourite necklace to pay a gambling debt.

"As he grew older he grew worse. He seduced women and abandoned them. He cared for nothing and nobody but himself, his own pleasure, his own chance to make money.

"Money. That was his god. I saw it but could do nothing about it. Finally he made the country too hot to hold him. He was clever with figures and he went to work for a financier. The man liked him, took him into his family. He thought Franklin was an orphan.

"Then he died in mysterious circumstances. My son came to me in tears and threw himself on my mercy. He swore the death had been an accident, begged me to help him get away. God forgive me, I allowed myself to be persuaded for the sake of his mother's memory.

"I gave him enough money to get to Liverpool, and from there he sailed for America. A friend went with him and saw him aboard, otherwise I would never have known, because he has never sent me word of himself since.

"Still I deluded myself that he was essentially innocent. But then it was discovered that the dead man's widow and children had been left destitute. The money that should have provided for them had vanished.

"In America he made such a name for himself as a

ruthless financier and railway entrepreneur that his legend became known over here."

"But how did you know that Jeremiah Wyngate was Franklin Tandy?" asked Rena.

"My wife had a great grandfather called Wyngate, a character so rough and unpleasant that tales of him reached down four generations. Of course he was the one Franklin admired. He must have felt safe enough taking his name. He was thousands of miles away from anyone who could have made the link.

"But I knew. Whenever tales of Jeremiah Wyngate's cruelty reached this country, I recognised my son."

The old man dropped his head into his hands and wept.

Instantly they were beside him. John, the frank and open-hearted man, took the old man into his arms and soothed him.

"Forgive me," Adolphus said, wiping his eyes. "I am unused to a sympathetic audience. I spend my life alone, these days. I find it hard to go out among my fellow man, because of my guilt."

"You bear no guilt," said John robustly.

"I think I do. I am guilty of having shielded him when I should have handed him over to the law. When I think of how many lives he's smashed and ruined since then my guilt is heavy indeed.

"But more than that, I feel guilty at having brought this creature into the world, and made the world a worse place."

"Did you know that he was here?" asked Rena.

"Not until after I had arrived in the village. I came at first for the pleasure of seeing John again, and helping him solve the mystery of these coins. It was only after I reached here that I sensed the stain that creature leaves wherever he goes.

"And then I heard that his daughter was with him – "

129

"The daughter that you used to watch in the park," said Rena, smiling.

"That's right. When I heard that he'd returned to London I couldn't bring myself to go and see him. It was better not to revive the past. But I used to watch his house sometimes, and I saw the little girl come out with her governess. I guessed who she was because she had a slight resemblance to Jane. That was how I knew I had a grand daughter."

"She remembers seeing you," said Rena. "I'm sure she'll be glad to meet you properly."

"I don't think that man will allow that. He was very determined to get rid of me when he saw me this morning."

"Why didn't you come to the house when he'd gone?" asked John.

"You can never be quite certain when he has gone," said Adolphus. "I waited a long time out there in the grounds, and I saw a young woman and a young man arrive. Was she – ?"

"Yes, that's Matilda," said Rena, "and the splendid young man with her is Cecil. They're in love and they want to marry, if they can escape her father."

"Heaven help them!" said Adolphus. "Or maybe they need some help a little closer to home. Does my son know about him?"

"He knows that he exists," said Rena, "and he's done everything he could to separate them, including having him dreadfully beaten by thugs. But he doesn't know that he's here now."

Something in her voice made Adolphus look at her closely. "When you say 'here' – ?"

"Here," said Rena. "In this house. We're hiding him upstairs."

"Well done, my dear."

"But it doesn't really help, does it?" she said. "Matilda asked us to allow Mr. Wyngate to come here, so that she could come too, but where is it all going to end?"

"Badly, I'm afraid," Adolphus said somberly. "I was watching as you all went up the tower. I couldn't hear what he said, but I saw his manner of saying it.

"And the devil took him up into a high place, and showed him the kingdoms of the world, and said all these will I give to thee, if thou wilt fall down and worship me."

"Yes," John said grimly. "That's just how it was. All the kingdoms of the world. He thinks they're his to give or withhold."

Adolphus was silent for a while. Then he said heavily, "I wonder if you're aware of his latest tactic. The rumour is going around the village that his money is being poured into this place, and of course everyone is rejoicing."

John groaned and dropped his head into his hands.

"How do I face them and tell them it won't happen?" he said. "In fact how do I fight Wyngate? What do you do with a man who doesn't understand the word 'no'."

"It's very simple," Adolphus said gently. "We pray for a miracle."

*

Next morning Rena introduced Adolphus to Cecil and had the pleasure of seeing that the two men liked each other.

"He's a fine young man," Adolphus confided to Rena. "Brave and hard working. He showed me some of his scars from the beating. My goodness if he wasn't put off by that then he's very much in love with her."

After breakfast he asked to be shown the place where the cross had stood and the coins had been found. John and Rena took him down to the woods to the place where the great ugly hole was still visible, and he looked at it for a long time, murmuring, "Hmm!"

Then, with a strength that belied his years, he got down and rooted around in the earth, finally getting to his feet, gasping and brushing himself down.

"And you say he was watching you?"

"I'm certain of it," Rena said.

"Then there won't be anything left here. That's his way. What became of the cross?"

They showed it to him lying on the ground, and he immediately bent to lift it.

"Take the other end," he roared to John.

Between them they carried the post back to its original position and slammed it back into the ground, deep enough to stand upright. When they had packed the earth back around it and stamped it down, it seemed secure again.

"I'm so glad," Rena said quietly. "That was how Papa wanted it to be."

It was as though this old man had blown a trumpet, heralding battle.

Adolphus looked at her kindly.

"Is there a chapel in this place?" he asked.

"Yes, Papa conducted the last Earl's funeral there."

"Would you be kind enough to show it to me?"

She led the way back into the house and round to the east wing, where there was a tiny chapel.

"Charming," Adolphus said. "Just the place for a quiet service. But I suppose it's been deconsecrated."

"Oh no," she said quickly. "Papa would never hear of it. He said the next Earl might appear at any time, and the chapel must always be ready for him."

"Thank you, my dear."

Slowly he walked forward to the altar, and knelt before it. There were no gorgeous ornaments on it now. They had been put into store, or perhaps sold.

But to Adolphus its shabbiness did not exist. To him this was a place of glory. Rena slipped into a pew behind him and said her own quiet prayer, that Wyngate might not prevail, that Matilda and Cecil might find a way to be together, and that the love she shared with John might prosper.

While she prayed she looked through her fingers at Adolphus. She couldn't have said why, but there was something about him that drew her gaze. To others he might look merely a shabby old man, but she sensed the presence of a mighty warrior.

And when he rose to his feet she knew he had come to a decision.

*

They returned to the kitchen to find John in a state of confusion. Several women from the village had confronted him, with their offerings.

"A loaf of bread for your lordship," the baker's wife was saying. She was one of the women who had nursed Rena through her illness, and her face brightened at the sight of her.

"And my husband would have me bring these ribs of beef," the butcher's wife put in quickly. "To welcome your lordship."

There were eight of them, and they had all brought something as a 'welcome'. Milk, cheese, butter, meat, these poor people were giving them enough to fill the larder for days. They had heard the rumours of coming prosperity, and wanted to know if they were true.

But part of them believed in good fortune against all odds, and this was their way of celebrating it.

Rena saw the blazing hope in their faces, and was sick at heart.

They took it for granted that she wanted the same thing that they did. What would they say if they knew she was the threat to their last hope?

Looking at John's face she saw that he too had

understood, and felt uneasy that he wasn't going to live up to their expectations.

When the last villager had gone, Adolphus said gently, "My son has done his work well, I see."

"They've been listening to the rumours he's spread," John said bitterly. "But what am I expected to do? I can't and won't marry Matilda, even if she was prepared to marry me. I should have just told them that Rena is to be my wife."

"No John," Rena said in a strained voice. "As you say, you can't marry Matilda, but that doesn't mean you can marry me. You have to think of them."

"Rena has this mad idea that I should put myself up for auction to some other heiress," John said angrily.

"You might – find one that you loved, and who loved you," she said. "If I wasn't here – "

"You or nobody," said John bluntly. "Adolphus, tell her she's talking nonsense."

"But perhaps she isn't," Adolphus said gently.

John was pale. "You can't mean that."

"I know that Rena will never do anything against her conscience," Adolphus said. "And you mustn't try to force her." He smiled at them both. "But we don't yet know what her conscience will say."

"But we do, we do," she said desperately.

"Have you forgotten my miracle," he asked, "or don't you believe in miracles?"

"I don't believe miracles happen to order, just because you want them," she said. "Oh, please I – "

Suddenly she felt she had to be alone.

"I must do some shopping," she said in a strained voice.

"After all this?" John asked, indicating the goods on the table.

"I still need more milk," she said hurriedly. "There are four of us living here now. I'll be back."

She ran out before they could detain her. Adolphus' words had caused a terrible pain in her heart. He was kind and gentle, and yet she could tell that he thought she was right. He would support her in her agonising decision, but he would not tell her to avoid it.

Wherever she went in the village she was met by smiling faces, inviting her to share their hope and joy. She smiled back and hurried on.

In the dairy she bought more milk and hurried out, hoping not to have to talk, but in the doorway she was stopped by an imposing figure.

"Mr. Daykers," she said. "Good morning."

"A word with you, Miss Colwell."

"I really am rather – "

"Kindly hear me out."

He stood in her path, sallow, domineering, with something brutal in his quiet manner.

"It is your future that I am here to discuss," he said.

"Once and for all, Mr. Daykers, I will not be your housekeeper."

"No, that would be ineligible. In view of this latest development I see that stronger measures are called for."

He took a deep breath and settled himself as though taking root in the ground.

"I offer myself to you in marriage."

"I – beg your pardon?"

"It must be clear to you that you can no longer remain in that house when a – ah – happy event has come to pass. Lord Lansdale knows his duty to the community, and you, I believe, are also conscious of your duty."

"You are very kind sir, but I have no desire for

marriage."

"You do not know the world young woman. You are living in a disgraceful situation, and should quit it without delay. Only an immediate marriage will rescue your reputation, and it is highly unlikely that you will ever find another man ready to sacrifice himself."

"You must excuse me, sir," she said breathlessly, "I have to go. I thank you for your offer but regret it is quite out of my power to accept it. Please stand aside."

When he remained before her she dodged round him and began to run. She ran and ran until she was out of sight, hidden in the woods on John's land.

There she stopped, leaning against a tree, gasping.

This was it. This was now the choice that life would offer her. After knowing the glory of John's love she was told she had no option but to become the wife of this pompous bully.

She must turn away from the only happiness she would ever know, and settle for a bitter, mean marriage to a man she could never like.

She could and would refuse to marry Steven Daykers, but without the man she loved all other choices would be equally wretched. And this would be her life, unless Adolphus could find a miracle.

But she no longer had faith in miracles.

Burying her face in her hands she slid slowly down the tree until she was on the ground, and sat there in a huddle while she sobbed and sobbed.

CHAPTER TEN

As Rena made her way to the house she became aware of a commotion going on. From inside came whoops of glee, laughter, triumph.

Then John came flying out.

"Rena," he called, waving and running to her.

"What's happened?" she asked as he whirled her around.

"Adolphus has made an incredible discovery. You remember that leather purse that we found under the cross?"

"The one that contained the last two coins, yes?"

"There was something else in it. A piece of paper. It's a riddle, a clue to the other twenty three coins. Adolphus thinks they're somewhere in the house and if we can find them – "

"Oh John, John can it really be true?"

"It has to be true. Don't you see, this is the miracle he spoke of. Come on."

He seized her hand and they ran back together.

Adolphus and Cecil were both hard at work in the picture gallery, covered in dust but cheerful and determined. Adolphus showed her the paper they had found.

"The leather has kept it in good condition," he said, "so it's still readable."

"Only to you," John said good humouredly. "It takes a scholar to read this."

"It must date from hundreds of years ago," Rena agreed. "That isn't modern English."

Adolphus nodded. "Written about the time of King

Charles II, I would say."

"And there's something about a King here." She was squinting at the paper. "What does it mean?"

"They were the King's coins, and the rest are to be found in some part of the house that is connected with him," said John. "So we started with the gallery because there are several portraits here of Charles II, and a couple where he appears with the family."

"So far we haven't been lucky," said Adolphus. "The coins aren't hidden behind them or anything. But we're not giving up."

To be on the verge of success and yet have it keep elusively out of reach made Rena feel giddy.

She fixed her eyes on one of the portraits that Adolphus showed her. It showed the king, still a young man, probably soon after his accession to the throne, sitting beside a window, gazing out onto a country scene. In his hands he held some gold coins.

"Would they be the coins that we are looking for?" she asked.

"Quite possibly," said Adolphus.

"Then perhaps we should be looking in the room depicted behind him," she said excitedly. "I know which one it is. I recognise the view. I've been going through the house recently and there's only one bedroom that shows you the land from exactly that angle. It was probably where the king slept when he stayed here."

"Can you take us to it?" asked John.

They followed her out into the hall and up the stairs. Then, to her horror, she found that her mind went blank. Suddenly all rooms and all corridors seemed alike.

"I can't remember," she whispered. "It's like being in a maze."

"Calmly now," Adolphus said, taking her hands. "You

are overwrought and that has confused your mind. The memory will return in a moment."

"Yes, yes," she said in relief as the jumble in her head began to sort itself out. "It's along here."

At the end of a long corridor they found the room. It was dirty and tattered, but at one time it must have been glorious. In the centre stood a huge four poster bed, its hangings crumbling, its decorations almost obscured by grime.

But one thing was still clear, the great crest that proclaimed that this bed was for the use of King Charles II. This had been his room, and of all rooms, surely it was the one most likely to hide the treasure they sought?

They began going through drawers and chests, looking for concealed cupboards behind hangings.

"But I fear it won't be hidden as obviously as that," said Adolphus. "We shall have to be subtle. What was that noise?"

They all listened and could hear the sound of carriage wheels, then Wyngate's ugly voice barking instructions.

"Has he dared – ?" John breathed.

"Of course," said Adolphus "Go down to him and distract his attention. Rena, you go down too. At all costs he must suspect nothing."

There was no choice but to do as he said. Together they descended the stairs to find the hallway a scene of chaos.

In the centre stood Wyngate and Matilda. Around them swarmed workmen, hurrying here and there, inspecting, grimacing at what they found.

"What is this?" John demanded.

Wyngate gave him a sour smile.

"I thought it was time to make a start."

"A start which I have not authorised," said John angrily.

"Come now, we know you're only playing games. You need what I have, and it's no use pretending otherwise. This work has to be done, and now is as good a time as any."

John's hands clenched at his side. In another moment he would have thrown Wyngate out bodily, but Rena's gentle touch made him stop and remember Adolphus' advice.

"Miss Wyngate," Rena said, stepping forward, "how nice to see you. Why don't you come with me and – ?"

Still talking she led Matilda away up the stairs.

"Is Cecil still here?" she whispered when they were a safe distance.

"Yes, I'm taking you to him. And somebody else is here. Your grandfather."

"I have no grandfather."

"But you have, and he is longing to see you."

They had reached the king's room and Rena threw open the door. Adolphus was studying a small cupboard. He looked up at the sound.

Then he became very still.

Tears began to pour down his face.

"Jane," he whispered. "My Jane."

"Jane was his wife," said Rena. "You look like your grandmother."

"You're the man I saw all those years ago," Matilda said suddenly. "I thought you were my father's ghost – you look so alike."

"No ghost, my dear," said Adolphus. "Just a man who had just discovered that he had a grandchild. I have always wanted to meet you properly." Tears still coursed down his cheeks, but he was smiling through them.

Matilda gave a little gasp and ran into his arms. She

too was weeping with joy.

"Grandfather, Grandfather," she cried.

He looked tenderly down at her face. "I thought you had something of the look of Jane, all those years ago," he said. "But you were a child, and it wasn't very clear. But now, it is like seeing my darling again."

"Papa always says I'm nothing to look at."

"You are beautiful," said Adolphus. "Cecil and I agree on that."

Now Matilda saw Cecil, watching them. Adolphus smiled as they hugged each other, and said, "I congratulate you on your choice of husband. He is an excellent young man."

"Oh Grandpapa, will you help us?"

"With all my heart. But first we must conclude our search of the house."

"There are some old coins hidden somewhere in the house," explained Rena. "They used to belong to Charles II."

"Then surely they'll be in his chapel?" said Matilda.

Everyone stared at her.

"The King's Chapel," she added.

"There is no King's Chapel here," said Rena. "It's just an ordinary chapel."

"Well, there was this waiter who served Papa and me in the hotel last night. He was ever so old and he said he used to work here when he was a boy. According to him the family always called it the King's Chapel, because of Charles II. He made it sound like a big secret, a name that only the family used, because the 'lower orders' weren't good enough. So if the place has been empty for years I suppose nobody would know."

"Sweet heaven, is it possible?" exclaimed Adolphus.

Some footsteps in the corridor made them all alert, but

it was only John.

"I've left Mr. Wyngate barking orders to workmen," he said. "He's perfectly happy as long as nobody contradicts him, so I thought I'd slip away for a moment. Has anybody found anything."

Swiftly Rena explained about the King's Chapel.

"What marvellous luck if it's true," said John. "Let's go and find out. But we'll have to be careful. Wyngate mustn't see you, Adolphus, or Cecil. I'll go back and draw him off."

It went against the grain with him but he managed to smile as he returned to where Wyngate was still in the hall, giving orders to a thick set man.

"This is Simpkins, the architect I've employed," he said.

John suppressed a wince and held out his hand to Simpkins. "Delighted to meet you sir. We must have some discussions about what you're going to do in my house." He stressed 'my' very slightly.

Simpkins, a decent man, was beginning to sense that something wasn't quite right here. Wyngate had spoken as though the house was his. He looked uncertainly from one to the other.

"Are those plans you're holding?" asked John, indicating some scrolled papers Simpkins had in his hand.

"Yes, sir."

"Why don't we all look at them in the library?"

As he'd hoped, at this sign that he was being more 'reasonable' a self satisfied sneer settled over Wyngate's face, and he made no protest at being led away to the library.

Now, John thought, the others had the chance to come downstairs and go to the chapel without being seen.

The plans were excellent, all but the tower. If only he could afford to do this work himself he would be glad to employ Simpkins.

If only....

His mind flew to the others in the chapel, searching, searching, everyone's fate depending on it.

He forced himself to concentrate.

"This tower is impossible," he said. "You must strengthen the foundations first."

Simpkins gave a sigh of relief. "That's what I keep trying to – "

"Shut up, both of you," snarled Wyngate. "That tower is what I want, just as it is. And I want it now. If you think – what the devil are you doing here?"

The other two looked up to see Adolphus standing in the doorway, regarding his son with sad, terrible eyes.

"Because I have longed to see you again," he said.

"Well, I haven't longed to see you, and I don't want to see you. I told you yesterday to get out. Why do you pursue me?"

"Perhaps because you are my son, and despite everything, I still love you."

"Sentimental nonsense!" Wyngate said with a kind of soft savagery. "Stay away from me. I won't be haunted by you."

"But you are haunted by me," said Adolphus in the same melancholy tone. "In your mind I have haunted you more with every act of wickedness. That is why the sight of me is so intolerable to you."

"Get out of this house."

"That is for the owner to say," Adolphus said, meeting his eyes. "You are not the owner, and you never will ever be."

"You're wrong. I've never been defeated yet.

"He – " Wyngate shot out his arm towards John, "won't refuse me in the end. He can't afford to."

"You are mistaken," said Adolphus. "He can't afford not to refuse you."

John moved to join him in the doorway.

"Mr. Simpkins," he said, "if I am fortunate, you and I may talk another time. In the meantime, stay well clear of the tower."

"You take your orders from me," Wyngate flashed at the architect.

"Now, come along, sir," Simpkins soothed him. "You wouldn't like me to bring the house down about your ears, would you?"

John took the opportunity to draw Adolphus out of the room.

"I thought you were going to stay hidden," he murmured.

"I will not hide from my own son. Strange as it may seem, I still love him, even hope to reclaim him."

As they spoke they were heading towards the back of the house where the chapel was. Cecil, Matilda and Rena were hunting through it. It was a big job, although the chapel itself was small.

"Of course it might be up there," said John, pointing upwards to the gallery that ran along one side of the chapel. "How can we reach it?"

"It's not accessible from down here," said Rena. "It was where the servants used to sit. They came in by their own door at the back."

"We must search the main chapel thoroughly first," said Adolphus. "And consider the gallery afterwards."

To everyone's dismay a thorough search of the chapel revealed nothing.

"What lies through that door?" Adolphus asked Rena. "The vestry, I suppose."

"Yes, just a very tiny one. Papa used it when he conducted services here, when I was a child. That didn't happen very often. Apart from the old Earl's funeral he baptised two children, and conducted one marriage. It was the Earl's great niece and she asked me to be her bridesmaid. I was so excited."

As she spoke she was opening the door to the vestry. There was the little table, and on it the register of births, marriages and funerals, still open, her father's writing clearly visible.

"Let's look at this wall behind," said Adolphus. "It's exactly the kind of place where a concealed cupboard could be. Help me move the desk."

Together they tried to push it but the desk wouldn't move.

"It's stuck on something," said Adolphus. "There's a loose floorboard sticking up. Let me try to – "

He was working away at the floorboard until suddenly it came loose in his hand and he lifted it right out.

There, in the gap beneath, was a leather purse, like the one Rena and John had found under the cross, but larger.

"Adolphus – "

"Steady my dear, don't get your hopes up too soon."

But she couldn't help darting to the door and calling into the chapel,

"Come quickly. We've found something."

In a moment the others were all huddled in the little vestry, crowding round Adolphus as he opened the bag, thrust in his hand, took out the contents and laid them on the desk.

Gold coins. Twenty three of them.

"Have we found them?" Rena whispered.

"We have found them," said Adolphus. "The twenty-three remaining gold coins that once belonged to King Charles II."

"And does that mean – ?" John also did not dare voice his hopes.

"It means that you have all thirty," said Adolphus. "Part of this nation's history. And as you have the complete set, their value is fabulous."

"You said a hundred thousand?" John said. "Can it really be so much?"

"I can give you the name of a collector who has been seeking these for years," said Adolphus. "I have no doubt of what they are worth to him. You will soon be safe."

"Safe!"

They all said the word, looking at each other. Then they said it again, for it was suddenly the most beautiful word in the world.

"Why do you say 'will be safe'?" John wanted to know. "Surely we are safe now?"

"You will not be safe until you are legally married," said Adolphus. "And that should take place as soon as possible."

"But he will stop us," said Matilda. "Not John and Rena, but he'll find a way to prevent me marrying Cecil. He'll just drag me off to London."

"Not if you marry here and now," said Adolphus.

Again they exchanged glances. "But can we?" asked John.

"I am a minister of the church, retired but still in orders. This chapel is still consecrated, so you told me Miss Colwell."

"Of course. You mean that you were thinking of this even then?"

"I like to look far ahead."

"Will it be valid without witnesses?" Cecil wanted to know.

"But we have witnesses," said Adolphus. "Each of you will witness the marriage of the other. And if my son tries to make trouble I shall simply refer the matter to the local bishop, who will support me."

"You know Bishop Hoston?" asked Rena.

"Know him? I taught him at theological college. He used to borrow books from me. In fact, I think he still has one or two. So that's all taken care of. Matilda, are you legally of age?"

"I am twenty-four."

"And you?" he looked at Rena.

"I am twenty-two, and have no family."

"Then I can marry you now, if that is your wish."

"Yes!" The four of them said it together.

"Then bolt the doors," said Adolphus robustly. "Let no-one enter until our work is done."

They were the strangest wedding ceremonies Rena had ever seen, yet she had no doubt that they were safe in the hands of this holy man. Apart from her father, no man had ever impressed her so deeply with his power for good.

By common consent Matilda and Cecil married first, since they had the most to fear from her father. Or, as John put it to his beloved,

"Wyngate cannot harm us now."

They married with curtain rings which Adolphus 'just happened' to have slipped into his pocket, at about the same time that he asked Rena about the status of the chapel.

John stood groomsman to Cecil, and then he and Rena signed the register which they had found in the vestry only half an hour ago.

Then the newly married Cecil became groomsman to

the Earl, while Mrs. Cecil Jenkins was Rena's attendant, both of them covered with dust but full of joy.

"Wilt thou take this woman – ?"

"I will."

"Wilt thou take this man – obey him and serve him, love, honour and keep him – forsaking all other, keep thee only unto him, as long as ye both shall live."

With profound joy, Rena responded, "I will."

"With this ring, I thee wed – "

Before John could say more there was a thunderous knocking on the door outside.

"Let me in!" bawled Wyngate's voice.

The door shook under his assault. But it held.

John's hand tightened on his bride's in silent reassurance, while his voice continued steadily reciting his vows.

The noise retreated from the door, and they heard footsteps climbing. The next moment Wyngate had appeared in the gallery high above, his face contorted with rage. He could see them, but not get to them.

"Stop this!" he screamed. "I demand that you stop!"

"Never fear," said Adolphus. "He has no power here."

He raised his voice.

"Forasmuch as John and Rena have consented together in holy wedlock – "

"No–oh!" shrieked Wyngate.

Adolphus made his measured way through the words, almost as though he could not hear the howls of rage and frustration coming from above.

" – I pronounce that they be man and wife together."

Now Wyngate had stopped screaming. In the silence he sent them a look of such malevolent hatred that Rena was startled.

"You'll pay for this," he snarled. "You think you can defy me and get away with it? Nobody has ever done that. I'll ruin you."

"You cannot ruin us," John called up to him. "We no longer need your money to safeguard the people or restore the house."

"The house," sneered Wyngate. "You think you're going to enjoy the house? This should have been my house. Nobody shall take it from me."

He turned sharply and the next moment he was gone. Distantly they could hear the sound of voices, shouts of warning, Simpkins calling, "Not up there, sir. It isn't safe."

"The roof," said John.

Hastily Adolphus pulled back the bolts and they all rushed out. From the gallery Wyngate had a good head start, and they could already hear him above them.

The next moment something went flying down past the window, to land with a crash on the terrace outside.

"It's a piece of stone from the turrets," said John. "He must be trying to destroy the house. Rena, stay here. Don't go outside whatever you do. It isn't safe."

"I'm coming with you," she cried, fearful for him.

"No darling, I want you to stay here."

"But – "

He gave her a faint smile. "Only a few minutes ago you vowed to obey me. Where's Adolphus?"

"He's gone up ahead."

Another crash as more stone came down. John raced after Adolphus, but the old clergyman had already reached the roof ahead of him, and was standing, facing Wyngate.

"Get away from me," Wyngate shrieked.

"It is over, my son. You can harm these people no more. The Earl is married, your daughter is married, and they have gone beyond you."

"This is your doing."

"No, it is your doing. You have driven away everyone who loved you, until only I am left. I am still your father."

"Keep your distance from me," Wyngate repeated, taking a step backwards.

"Don't go too near the edge," Adolphus cried. "The stone is missing there."

"This is mine," Wyngate said fiercely. "I will not give it up. I shall fight them for it. Look out there – " he swept his arm out in the direction of the estate. "Land fit for a king. Fit for me. Mine. Mine!"

"Nothing is yours," said Adolphus. "You have thrown away everything that matters, and now nothing is left."

Silence.

Only the wind.

They faced each other over several feet. Neither moved, but Adolphus saw in his son's eyes that he had understood.

"Nothing – " Wyngate repeated hoarsely. "Nothing is mine. Nothing is left. Nothing."

He looked out over the inheritance he had fought so hard to steal, and which now would never be his.

The next moment he had vanished.

From below came shouts of horror as he dropped sixty feet to land on the flagstones below.

No man could survive such a fall.

John, bursting out onto the roof, saw Adolphus standing there, stock still, his eyes fixed bleakly on the distance.

"Adolphus, are you all right? Where is Wyngate."

"He fell," the old man said through his tears. "He was standing by the edge and – he fell."

Cautiously John went to the edge and looked over. Down below a crowd of workmen were standing in a circle around Wyngate, but still they kept their distance, as though even in death Wyngate was terrifying.

He lay on his back, staring up to the sky, his eyes open and blank.

John turned back to where Adolphus stood, still motionless.

"Let's go down," he said gently.

"He was my son," Adolphus said softly. "He was my son."

*

The coins fetched slightly more than Adolphus' prediction, and John immediately put the work in hand, not only on his own house but on the cottages that dotted the estate.

Now there was accommodation for his workers, and jobs for everyone who needed them. Mr. Simpkins was summoned back to do a new set of plans, and the house rang with the sound of workmen.

Best of all it was early enough in the year to revive the farms and sow this year's crops.

"There's a lot more to be done," the Earl of Lansdale told his Countess as they strolled together by the stream when the harvest had been gathered. "It wasn't a large harvest this year, because we were so short of time. But next year will be an even greater success."

"And the year after," said Rena, "and the year after that, and all the years to come. Nothing matters, except that we'll be together."

Their walk had brought them to the cross, sturdy and upright since a group of workmen had dug new foundations and settled it securely in the earth.

"I'm glad we asked Adolphus to bless it," said John.

151

"Yes, now it speaks of him as well as Papa."

"I think he's going to be all right."

"I'm sure he will," said Rena. "Matilda writes to me from London that for a while they feared for his reason, so deep was his grief. But when he knew that he was to be a great grandfather he came back to life.

"But what I think pleased him most was the news that Matilda planned to use only a small part of her vast inheritance, just enough to set Cecil up in his own business. The rest will go to making reparations to those her father injured. It was only then that Adolphus agreed to live with them."

"I had hoped to persuade him to spend a little time with us," said John.

"But of course," Rena assented eagerly. "Who else could baptise our child in the King's Chapel?"

"Our child," he said tenderly. "Are you quite certain?"

"Quite certain. In the spring. And then we will have everything."

"No," he said, taking her face between his hands. "When I think of what could have happened, how we might have lost each other, then I know that I have everything now. Whatever else befalls us in life, you and you alone are my everything. And that is how it will be forever."

"Forever," she murmured. "It has such a beautiful sound."

"Yes," he said. "And it will be beautiful, in this life and the next, because we will have the love that God gave us. Forever. Until the end of time."